Paddington

MICHAEL BOND

A Classic Collection

With drawings by Peggy Fortnum
Coloured by Caroline Nuttall-Smith

Collins
An Imprint of HarperCollinsPublishers

To Karen.
Like Paddington, she never ages.
MB

Please Look After this Bear and *A Shopping Expedition* from *A Bear Called Paddington*
First published in 1958 by William Collins & Co. Ltd
Trouble at the Launderette from *Paddington Helps Out*
First published in 1960 by William Collins & Co. Ltd
A Spot of Decorating, Paddington and the Bonfire and *Christmas* from *More About Paddington*
First published in 1959 by William Collins & Co. Ltd
Too Much Off the Top from *Paddington at Work*
First published in 1966 by William Collins & Co. Ltd
Paddington at the Wheel from *Paddington Takes the Test*
First published in 1979 by William Collins & Co. Ltd

First published in Great Britain in this volume in 1998 by Collins

Collins is an imprint of HarperCollins*Publishers* Ltd
77-85 Fulham Palace Road, Hammersmith,
London, W6 8JB

1 3 5 7 9 8 6 4 2

This edition text copyright © Michael Bond 1958, 1959, 1960, 1966
Illustrations copyright © Peggy Fortnum and
William Collins Sons & Co. Ltd 1958, 1959, 1960, 1966

ISBN 0 00 198 297-4

The author asserts the moral right to be identified as the author of the work.

Printed and bound in Italy

CONTENTS

Introduction

by Michael Bond

Someone once wrote to me saying that he was so used to Paddington being the name of a bear it now seemed a funny name for a railway station. I do know what was meant, for to me he has always been very real.

That's not so surprising, because if an author doesn't believe in his own characters, no one else is going to. "What would Paddington do?" I sometimes ask myself when confronted with a problem. "What would he think of it all?" And almost at once everything becomes clear.

The fact that over the past forty years many people the world over have clearly felt the same way about him has always given me great pleasure.

Bears don't have Ruby anniversaries, so here to celebrate what Paddington might call his *Marmalade* anniversary are eight of his favourite adventures.

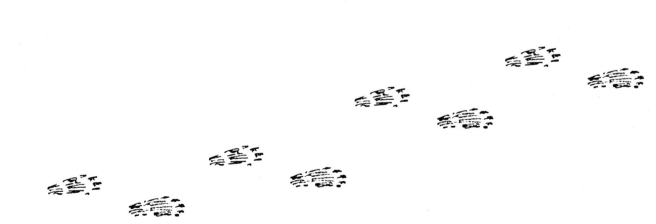

1

Please Look After this Bear

Mr and Mrs Brown first met Paddington on a railway platform. In fact, that was how he came to have such an unusual name for a bear, for Paddington was the name of the station.

The Browns were there to meet their daughter Judy, who was coming home from school for the holidays. It was a warm summer day and the station was crowded with people on their way to the seaside. Trains were humming, loudspeakers blaring, porters rushing about shouting at one another, and altogether there was so much noise that Mr Brown, who saw him first, had to tell his wife several times before she understood.

"A bear? On Paddington station?" Mrs Brown looked at her husband in amazement. "Don't be silly, Henry. There can't be!"

Mr Brown adjusted his glasses. "But there is," he insisted. "I distinctly saw it. Over there – near the bicycle rack. It was wearing a funny kind of hat."

Without waiting for a reply he caught hold of his wife's arm and pushed her through the crowd, round a trolley laden with chocolate and cups of tea, past a bookstall, and through a gap in a pile of suitcases towards the Lost Property Office.

"There you are," he announced triumphantly, pointing towards a dark corner, "I told you so!"

Mrs Brown followed the direction of his arm and dimly made out a small, furry object in the shadows. It seemed to be sitting on some kind of suitcase and around its neck there was a label with some writing on it. The suitcase was old and battered and on the side, in large letters, were the words WANTED ON VOYAGE.

Mrs Brown clutched at her husband. "Why, Henry," she exclaimed. "I believe you were right after all. It is a bear!"

She peered at it more closely. It seemed a very unusual kind of bear. It was brown in colour, a rather dirty brown, and it was wearing a most odd-looking hat, with a wide brim, just as Mr Brown had said. From beneath the brim two large, round eyes stared back at her.

Seeing that something was expected of it the bear stood up and politely raised its hat, revealing two black ears. "Good afternoon," it said, in a small, clear voice.

"Er... good afternoon," replied Mr Brown, doubtfully. There was a moment of silence.

The bear looked at them inquiringly. "Can I help you?"

Mr Brown looked rather embarrassed "Well... no. Er... as a matter of fact, we were wondering if we could help you."

Mrs Brown bent down. "You're a very small bear," she said.

The bear puffed out its chest. "I'm a very rare sort of bear," he replied importantly. "There aren't many of us left where I come from."

"And where is that?" asked Mrs Brown.

The bear looked round carefully before replying. "Darkest Peru. I'm not really supposed to be here at all. I'm a stowaway!"

"A stowaway?" Mr Brown lowered his voice and looked anxiously over his shoulder. He almost expected to see a policeman standing behind him with a notebook and pencil, taking everything down.

"Yes," said the bear. "I emigrated, you know." A sad expression came into its eyes. "I used to live with my Aunt Lucy in Peru, but she had to go into a home for retired bears."

"You don't mean to say you've come all the way from South America by yourself?" exclaimed Mrs Brown.

The bear nodded. "Aunt Lucy always said she wanted me to emigrate when I was old enough. That's why she taught me to speak English."

"But whatever did you do for food?" asked Mr Brown. "You must be starving."

Bending down, the bear unlocked the suitcase with a small key, which it also had round its neck, and brought out an almost empty glass jar. "I ate marmalade," he said, rather proudly. "Bears like marmalade. And I lived in a lifeboat."

"But what are you going to do now?" said Mr Brown. "You can't just sit on Paddington station waiting for something to happen."

"Oh, I shall be all right… I expect." The bear bent down to do up its case again. As he did so Mrs Brown caught a glimpse of the writing on the label. It said, simply, PLEASE LOOK AFTER THIS BEAR. THANK YOU.

She turned appealingly to her husband. "Oh, Henry, what shall we do? We can't just leave him here. There's no knowing what might happen to him. London's such a big place when you've nowhere to go. Can't he come and stay with us for a few days?"

Mr Brown hesitated. "But Mary, dear, we can't take him… not just like that. After all…"

"After all, what?" Mrs Brown's voice had a firm note to it. She looked down at the bear. "He is rather sweet. And he'd be such company for Jonathan and Judy. Even if it's only for a little while. They'd never forgive us if they knew you'd left him here."

"It all seems highly irregular," said Mr Brown, doubtfully. "I'm sure there's a law about it." He bent down. "Would you like to come and stay with us?" he asked. "That is," he added, hastily, not wishing to offend the bear, "if you've nothing else planned."

The bear jumped and his hat nearly fell off with excitement. "Oooh, yes, please. I should like that very much. I've nowhere to go and everyone seems in such a hurry."

"Well, that's settled then," said Mrs Brown, before her husband could change his mind. "And you can have marmalade for breakfast every morning, and – " she tried hard to think of something else that bears might like.

"Every morning?" The bear looked as if it could hardly believe its ears. "I only had it on special occasions at home. Marmalade's very expensive in Darkest Peru."

"Then you shall have it every morning starting tomorrow," continued Mrs Brown. "And honey on Sunday."

A worried expression came over the bear's face. "Will it cost very much?" he asked. "You see, I haven't very much money."

"Of course not. We wouldn't dream of charging you anything. We shall expect you to be one of the family, shan't we, Henry?" Mrs Brown looked at her husband for support.

"Of course," said Mr Brown. "By the way," he added, "if you are coming home with us you'd better know our names. This is Mrs Brown and I'm Mr Brown."

The bear raised its hat politely – twice. "I haven't really got a name," he said. "Only a Peruvian one which no one can understand."

"Then we'd better give you an English one," said Mrs Brown. "It'll make things much easier." She looked round the station for inspiration. "It ought to be something special," she said thoughtfully. As she spoke an engine standing in one of the platforms gave a loud wail and a train began to move. "I know what!" she exclaimed. "We found you in Paddington station so we'll call you Paddington!"

"Paddington!" The bear repeated it several times to make sure. "It seems a very long name."

"Quite distinguished," said Mr Brown. "Yes, I like Paddington as a name. Paddington it shall be."

Mrs Brown stood up. "Good. Now, Paddington, I have to meet our little daughter, Judy, off the train. She's coming home from school. I'm sure you must be thirsty after your long journey, so you go along to the buffet with Mr Brown and he'll buy you a nice cup of tea."

Paddington licked his lips. "I'm very thirsty," he said. "Sea water makes you thirsty." He picked up his suitcase, pulled his hat down firmly over his head, and waved a paw politely in the direction of the buffet. "After you, Mr Brown."

"Er… thank you, Paddington," said Mr Brown.

"Now, Henry, look after him," Mrs Brown called after them. "And for goodness' sake, when you get a moment, take that label off his neck. It makes him look like a parcel. I'm sure he'll get put in a luggage van or something if a porter sees him."

The buffet was crowded when they entered but Mr Brown managed to find a table for two in a corner. By standing on a chair Paddington could just rest his paws comfortably on the glass top. He looked around with interest while Mr Brown went to fetch the tea. The sight of everyone eating reminded him of how hungry he felt. There was a half-eaten bun on the table but just as he reached out his paw a waitress came up and swept it into a pan.

"You don't want that, dearie," she said, giving him a friendly pat. "You don't know where it's been."

Paddington felt so empty he didn't really mind where it had been but he was much too polite to say anything.

"Well, Paddington," said Mr Brown, as he placed two steaming cups of tea on the table and a plate piled high with cakes. "How's that to be going on with?"

Paddington's eyes glistened. "It's very nice, thank you," he exclaimed, eyeing the tea doubtfully. "But it's rather hard drinking out of a cup. I usually get my head stuck, or else my hat falls in and makes it taste nasty."

Mr Brown hesitated. "Then you'd better give your hat to me. I'll pour the tea into a saucer for you. It's not really done in the best circles, but I'm sure no one will mind just this once."

Paddington removed his hat and laid it carefully on the table while Mr Brown poured out the tea. He looked hungrily at the cakes, in particular at a large cream-and-jam one which Mr Brown placed on a plate in front of him.

"There you are, Paddington," he said. "I'm sorry they haven't any marmalade ones, but they were the best I could get."

"I'm glad I emigrated," said Paddington, as he reached out a paw and pulled the plate nearer. "Do you think anyone would mind if I stood on the table to eat?"

Before Mr Brown could answer he had climbed up and placed his right paw firmly on the bun. It was a very large bun, the biggest and stickiest Mr Brown had been able to find, and in a matter of moments most of the inside found its way on to Paddington's whiskers. People started to nudge each other and began staring in their direction. Mr Brown wished he had chosen a plain, ordinary bun, but he wasn't very experienced in the ways of bears. He stirred his tea and looked out of the window, pretending he had tea with a bear in Paddington station every day of his life.

"Henry!" The sound of his wife's voice brought him back to earth with a start. "Henry, whatever are you doing to that poor bear? Look at him! He's covered all over with cream and jam."

Mr Brown jumped up in confusion. "He seemed rather hungry," he answered, lamely.

Mrs Brown turned to her daughter. "This is what happens when I leave your father alone for five minutes."

Judy clapped her hands excitedly. "Oh, Daddy, is he really going to stay with us?"

"If he does," said Mrs Brown, "I can see someone other than your father will have to look after him. Just look at the mess he's in!"

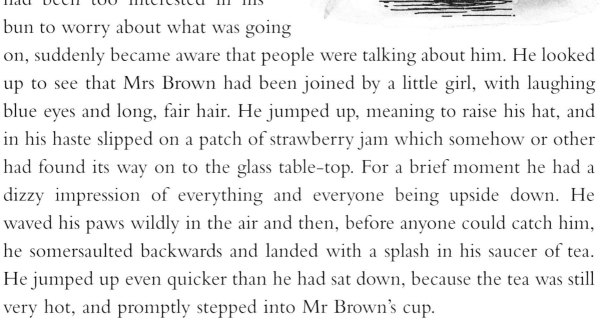

Paddington, who all this time had been too interested in his bun to worry about what was going on, suddenly became aware that people were talking about him. He looked up to see that Mrs Brown had been joined by a little girl, with laughing blue eyes and long, fair hair. He jumped up, meaning to raise his hat, and in his haste slipped on a patch of strawberry jam which somehow or other had found its way on to the glass table-top. For a brief moment he had a dizzy impression of everything and everyone being upside down. He waved his paws wildly in the air and then, before anyone could catch him, he somersaulted backwards and landed with a splash in his saucer of tea. He jumped up even quicker than he had sat down, because the tea was still very hot, and promptly stepped into Mr Brown's cup.

Judy threw back her head and laughed until the tears rolled down her face. "Oh, Mummy, isn't he funny!" she cried.

Paddington, who didn't think it at all funny, stood for a moment with one foot on the table and the other in Mr Brown's tea. There were large patches of white cream all over his face, and on his left ear there was a lump of strawberry jam.

"You wouldn't think," said Mrs Brown, "that anyone could get in such a state with just one bun."

Mr Brown coughed. He had just caught the stern eye of a waitress on the other side of the counter. "Perhaps," he said, "we'd better go. I'll see if I can find a taxi." He picked up Judy's belongings and hurried outside.

Paddington stepped gingerly off the table and, with a last look at the sticky remains of his bun, climbed down on to the floor.

Judy took one of his paws. "Come along, Paddington. We'll take you home and you can have a nice hot bath. Then you can tell me all about South America. I'm sure you must have had lots of wonderful adventures."

"I have," said Paddington earnestly. "Lots. Things are always happening to me. I'm that sort of bear."

When they came out of the buffet Mr Brown had already found a taxi and he waved them across. The driver looked hard at Paddington and then at the inside of his nice, clean taxi.

"Bears is extra," he said gruffly. "Sticky bears is twice as much again."

"He can't help being sticky, driver," said Mr Brown. "He's just had a nasty accident."

The driver hesitated. "All right, 'op in. But mind none of it comes off on me interior. I only cleaned it out this morning."

The Browns trooped obediently into the back of the taxi. Mr and Mrs Brown and Judy sat in the back, while Paddington stood on a tip-up seat behind the driver so that he could see out of the window.

The sun was shining as they drove out of the station and after the gloom and the noise everything seemed bright and cheerful. They swept past a group of people at a bus stop and Paddington waved. Several people stared and one man raised his hat in return. It was all very friendly. After weeks of sitting alone in a lifeboat there was so much to see. There were people and cars and big, red buses everywhere – it wasn't a bit like Darkest Peru.

Paddington kept one eye out of the window in case he missed anything. With his other eye he carefully examined Mr and Mrs Brown and Judy. Mr Brown was fat and jolly, with a big moustache and glasses, while Mrs Brown, who was also rather plump, looked like a larger edition of Judy. Paddington had just decided he was going to like staying with the Browns when the glass window behind the driver shot back and a gruff voice said, "Where did you say you wanted to go?"

Mr Brown leaned forward. "Number thirty-two, Windsor Gardens."

The driver cupped his ear with one hand. "Can't 'ear you," he shouted.

Paddington tapped him on the shoulder. "Number thirty-two, Windsor Gardens," he repeated.

The taxi driver jumped at the sound of Paddington's voice and narrowly missed hitting a bus. He looked down at his shoulder and glared. "Cream!" he said, bitterly. "All over me new coat!"

Judy giggled and Mr and Mrs Brown exchanged glances. Mr Brown peered at the meter. He half expected to see a sign go up saying they had to pay another fifty pence.

"I beg your pardon," said Paddington. He bent forward and tried to rub the stain off with his other paw. Several bun crumbs and a smear of jam added themselves mysteriously to the taxi driver's coat. The driver gave Paddington a long, hard look. Paddington raised his hat and the driver slammed the window shut again.

"Oh dear," said Mrs Brown. "We really shall have to give him a bath as soon as we get indoors. It's getting everywhere."

Paddington looked thoughtful. It wasn't so much that he didn't like baths; he really didn't mind being covered with jam and cream. It seemed a pity to wash it all off quite so soon. But before he had time to consider the matter the taxi stopped and the Browns began to climb out. Paddington picked up his suitcase and followed Judy up a flight of white steps to a big green door.

"Now you're going to meet Mrs Bird," said Judy. "She looks after us. She's a bit fierce sometimes and she grumbles a lot but she doesn't really mean it. I'm sure you'll like her."

Paddington felt his knees begin to tremble. He looked round for Mr and Mrs Brown, but they appeared to be having some sort of argument with the taxi driver. Behind the door he could hear footsteps approaching.

"I'm sure I shall like her, if you say so," he said, catching sight of his reflection on the brightly polished letterbox. "But will she like me?"

2

A Shopping Expedition

The man in the gentlemen's outfitting department at Barkridges held Paddington's hat at arm's length between thumb and forefinger. He looked at it distastefully.

"I take it the young… er, gentleman, will not be requiring this any more, Modom?" he said.

"Oh yes, I shall," said Paddington firmly. "I've always had that hat – ever since I was small."

"But wouldn't you like a nice new one, Paddington?" said Mrs Brown hastily, "for best?"

Paddington thought for a moment. "I'll have one for worst if you like," he said. "That's my best one!"

The salesman shuddered slightly and, averting his gaze, placed the offending article on the far end of the counter.

"Albert!" He beckoned to a youth who was hovering in the background. "See what we have in size $4\frac{7}{8}$." Albert began to rummage under the counter.

"And now, while we're about it," said Mrs Brown, "we'd like a nice warm coat for the winter. Something like a duffle coat with toggles so that he can do it up easily, I thought. And we'd also like a plastic raincoat for the summer."

The salesman looked at her haughtily. He wasn't very fond of bears and this one, especially, had been giving him odd looks ever since he'd mentioned his wretched hat. "Has Modom tried the bargain basement?" he began. "Something in Government Surplus…"

"No, I haven't," said Mrs Brown, hotly. "Government Surplus indeed! I've never heard of such a thing – have you, Paddington?"

"No," said Paddington, who had no idea what Government Surplus was. "Never!" He stared hard at the man, who looked away uneasily. Paddington had a very persistent stare when he cared to use it. It was a very powerful stare. One which his Aunt Lucy had taught him and which he kept for special occasions.

Mrs Brown pointed to a smart blue duffle coat with a red lining. "That looks the very thing," she said.

The assistant gulped. "Yes, Modom. Certainly, Modom." He beckoned to Paddington. "Come this way, sir."

Paddington followed the assistant, keeping about two feet behind him, and staring very hard. The back of the man's neck seemed to go a dull red and he fingered his collar nervously. As they passed the hat counter, Albert, who lived in constant fear of his superior, and who had been watching the events with an open mouth, gave Paddington the thumbs-up sign. Paddington waved a paw. He was beginning to enjoy himself.

He allowed the assistant to help him on with the coat and then stood admiring himself in the mirror. It was the first coat he had ever possessed. In Peru it had been very hot, and though his Aunt Lucy had made him wear a hat to prevent sunstroke, it had always been much too warm for a coat of any sort. He looked at himself in the mirror and was surprised to see not one, but a long line of bears stretching away as far as the eye could see. In fact, everywhere he looked there were bears, and they were all looking extremely smart.

"Isn't the hood a trifle large?" asked Mrs Brown, anxiously.

"Hoods are being worn large this year, Modom," said the assistant. "It's the latest fashion." He was about to add that Paddington seemed to have rather a large head anyway but he changed his mind. Bears were rather unpredictable. You never quite knew what they were thinking and this one in particular seemed to have a mind of his own.

"Do you like it, Paddington?" asked Mrs Brown.

Paddington gave up counting bears in the mirror and turned round to look at the back view. "I think it's the nicest coat I've ever seen," he said, after a moment's thought. Mrs Brown and the assistant heaved a sigh of relief.

"Good," said Mrs Brown. "That's settled, then. Now there's just the question of a hat and a plastic macintosh."

She walked over to the hat counter, where Albert who could still hardly take his admiring eyes off Paddington, had arranged a huge pile of hats. There were bowler hats, sun hats, trilby hats, berets, and even a very small top hat. Mrs Brown eyed them doubtfully. "It's difficult," she said, looking at Paddington. "It's largely a question of his ears. They stick out rather."

"You could cut some holes for them," said Albert.

The assistant froze him with a glance. "Cut a hole in a Barkridges' hat!" he exclaimed. "I've never heard of such a thing."

Paddington turned and stared at him. "I... er..." The assistant's voice trailed off. "I'll go and fetch my scissors," he said, in a strange voice.

"I don't think that will be necessary at all," said Mrs Brown, hurriedly. "It's not as if he had to go to work in the city, so he doesn't want anything too smart. I think this woollen beret is very nice. The one with the pom-pom on top. The green will go well with his new coat and it'll stretch so that he can pull it down over his ears when it gets cold."

Everyone agreed that Paddington looked very smart, and while Mrs Brown looked for a plastic macintosh, he trotted off to have another look at himself in the mirror. He found the beret was a little difficult to raise as his ears kept the bottom half firmly in place. But by pulling on the pom-pom he could make it stretch quite a long way, which was almost as good. It meant, too, that he could be polite without getting his ears cold.

The assistant wanted to wrap up the duffle coat for him but after a lot of fuss it was agreed that, even though it was a warm day, he should wear it. Paddington felt very proud of himself and he was anxious to see if other people noticed.

After shaking hands with Albert, Paddington gave the assistant one more long, hard stare and the unfortunate man collapsed into a chair and began mopping his brow as Mrs Brown led the way out through the door.

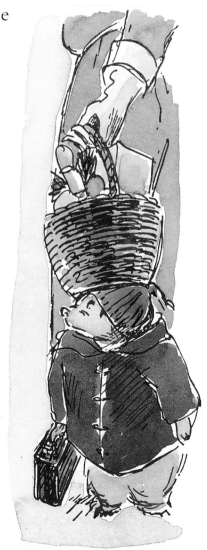

Barkridges was a large shop and it even had its own escalator as well as several lifts. Mrs Brown hesitated at the door and then took Paddington's paw firmly in her hand and led him towards the lift. She'd had enough of escalators for one day.

But to Paddington everything was new, or almost everything, and he liked trying strange things. After a few seconds he decided quite definitely that he preferred riding on an escalator. They were nice and smooth. But lifts! To start with, it was full of people carrying parcels and all so busy they had not time to notice a small bear — one woman even rested her shopping bag on his head and seemed quite surprised when Paddington pushed it off. Then suddenly half of him seemed to fall away while the other half stayed where it was. Just as he had got used to that feeling the second half of him caught up again and even overtook the first half before the doors opened. It did that four times on the way down and Paddington was glad when the man in charge said it was the ground floor and Mrs Brown led him out.

She looked at him closely. "Oh dear, Paddington, you look quite pale," she said. "Are you all right?"

"I feel sick," said Paddington. "I don't like lifts. And I wish I hadn't had such a big breakfast!"

"Oh dear!" Mrs Brown looked around. Judy, who had gone off to do some shopping on her own, was nowhere to be seen. "Will you be all right sitting here for a few minutes while I go off to find Judy?" she asked.

Paddington sank down on to his case looking very mournful. Even the pom-pom on his hat seemed limp.

"I don't know whether I shall be all right," he said. "But I'll do my best."

"I'll be as quick as I can," said Mrs Brown. "Then we can take a taxi home for lunch."

Paddington groaned. "Poor Paddington," said Mrs Brown, "you must be feeling bad if you don't want any lunch." At the word lunch again, Paddington closed his eyes and gave an even louder groan. Mrs Brown tiptoed away.

Paddington kept his eyes closed for several minutes and then, as he began to feel better, he gradually became aware that every now and then a nice cool draught of air blew over his face. He opened one eye carefully to see where it was coming from and noticed for the first time that he was sitting near the main entrance to the shop. He opened his other eye and decided to investigate. If he stayed just outside the glass door he could still see Mrs Brown and Judy when they came.

And then, as he bent down to pick up his suitcase, everything suddenly went black. "Oh dear," thought Paddington, "now all the lights have gone out."

He began groping his way with outstretched paws towards the door. He gave a push where he thought it ought to be but nothing happened. He tried moving along the wall a little way and gave another push. This time it did move. The door seemed to have a strong spring on it and he had to push hard to make it open but eventually there was a gap big enough for him to squeeze through. It clanged shut behind him and Paddington was disappointed to find it was just as dark outside as it had been in the shop. He began to wish he'd stayed where he was. He turned round and tried to find the door but it seemed to have disappeared.

He decided it might be easier if he got down on his paws and crawled. He went a little way like this and then his head came up against something hard. He tried to push it to one side with his paw and it moved slightly so he pushed again.

Suddenly, there was a noise like thunder, and before he knew where he was a whole mountain of things began to fall on him. It felt as if the whole sky had fallen in. Everything went quiet and he lay where he was for a few minutes with his eyes tightly shut, hardly daring to breathe. From a long way away he could hear voices and once or twice it sounded as if someone was banging on a window. He opened one eye carefully and was surprised to find the lights had come on again. At least…

Sheepishly he pushed the hood of his duffle coat up over his head. They hadn't gone out at all! His hood must have fallen over his head when he bent down inside the shop to pick up his case.

Paddington sat up and looked around to see where he was. He felt much better now. Somewhat to his astonishment, he found he was sitting in a small room in the middle of which was a great pile of tins and basins and bowls. He rubbed his eyes and stared, round-eyed, at the sight.

Behind him there was a wall with a door in it, and in front of him there was a large window. On the other side of the window there was a large crowd of people pushing one another and pointing in his direction. Paddington decided with pleasure that they must be pointing at him. He stood up with difficulty, because it was hard standing up straight on top of a lot of tins, and pulled the pom-pom on his hat as high as it would go. A cheer went up from the crowd. Paddington gave a bow, waved several times, and then started to examine the damage all around him.

For a moment he wasn't quite sure where he was, and then it came to him. Instead of going out into the street he must have opened a door leading to one of the shop windows!

Paddington was an observant bear, and since he had arrived in London he'd noticed lots of these shop windows. They were very interesting. They always had so many things inside them to look at. Once, he'd seen a man working in one, piling tin cans and boxes on top of each other to make a pyramid. He remembered deciding at the time what a nice job it must be.

He looked around thoughtfully. "Oh dear," he said to the world in general, "I'm in trouble again." If he'd knocked all these things down, as he supposed he must have done, someone was going to be cross. In fact, lots of people were going to be cross. People weren't very good at having things explained to them and it was going to be difficult explaining how his duffle coat hood had fallen over his head.

He bent down and began to pick up the things. There were some glass shelves lying on the floor where they had fallen. It was getting warm inside the window so he took off his duffle coat and hung it carefully on a nail. Then he picked up a glass shelf and tried balancing it on top of some tins.

It seemed to work so he put some more tins and a washing-up bowl on top of that. It was rather wobbly but… he stood back and examined it… yes, it looked quite nice. There was an encouraging round of applause from outside. Paddington waved a paw at the crowd and picked up another shelf.

Inside the shop, Mrs Brown was having an earnest conversation with the store detective.

"You say you left him here, Madam?" the detective was saying.

"That's right," said Mrs Brown. "He was feeling ill and I told him not to go away. His name's Paddington."

"Paddington." The detective wrote it carefully in his notebook. "What sort of bear is he?"

"Oh, he's sort of golden," said Mrs Brown. "He was wearing a blue duffle coat and carrying a suitcase."

"And he has black ears," said Judy. "You can't mistake him."

"Black ears," the detective repeated, licking his pencil.

"I don't expect that'll help much," said Mrs Brown. "He was wearing his beret."

The detective cupped his hand over his ear. "His what?" he shouted. There really was a terrible noise coming from somewhere. It seemed to be getting worse every minute. Every now and then there was a round of applause and several times he distinctly heard the sound of people cheering.

"His beret," shouted Mrs Brown in return. "A green woollen one that came down over his ears. With a pom-pom."

The detective shut his notebook with a snap. The noise outside was definitely getting worse. "Pardon me," he said, sternly. "There's something strange going on that needs investigating."

Mrs Brown and Judy exchanged glances. The same thought was running through both their minds. They both said, "Paddington!" and rushed after the detective. Mrs Brown clung to the detective's coat and Judy clung to Mrs Brown's as they forced their way through the crowd on the pavement. Just as they reached the window a tremendous cheer went up.

"I might have known," said Mrs Brown.

"Paddington!" exclaimed Judy.

Paddington had just reached the top of his pyramid. At least, it had started off to be a pyramid, but it wasn't really. It wasn't any particular shape at all and it was very rickety. Having placed the last tin on the top, Paddington was in trouble. He wanted to get down but he couldn't. He reached out a paw and the mountain began to wobble. Paddington clung helplessly to the tins, swaying to and fro, watched by a fascinated audience. And then, without any warning, the whole lot collapsed again, only this time Paddington was on top and not underneath. A groan of disappointment went up from the crowd.

"Best thing I've seen in years," said a man in the crowd to Mrs Brown. "Blessed if I know how they think these things up."

"Will he do it again, Mummy?" asked a small boy.

"I don't think so, dear," said his mother. "I think he's finished for the day." She pointed to the window where the detective was removing a sorry-looking Paddington. Mrs Brown hurried back to the entrance followed by Judy.

Inside the shop the detective looked at Paddington and then at his notebook. "Blue duffle coat," he said. "Green woollen beret!" He pulled the beret off. "Black ears! I know who you are," he said grimly; "you're Paddington!"

Paddington nearly fell backwards with astonishment.

"However did you know that?" he said.

"I'm a detective," said the man. "It's my job to know these things. We're always on the look-out for criminals."

"But I'm not a criminal," said Paddington hotly. "I'm a bear! Besides,

I was only tidying up the window…"

"Tidying up the window," the detective spluttered. "I don't know what Mr Perkins will have to say. He only dressed it this morning."

Paddington looked round uneasily. He could see Mrs Brown and Judy hurrying towards him. In fact, there were several people coming his way, including an important-looking man in a black coat and striped trousers. They all reached him at the same time and all began talking together.

Paddington sat down on his case and watched them. There were times when it was much better to keep quiet, and this was one of them. In the end it was the important-looking man who won, because he had the loudest voice and kept on talking when everyone else had finished.

To Paddington's surprise he reached down, took hold of his paw, and started to shake it so hard he thought it was going to drop off.

"Delighted to know you, bear," he boomed. "Delighted to know you. And congratulations."

"That's all right," said Paddington, doubtfully. He didn't know why, but the man seemed very pleased.

The man turned to Mrs Brown. "You say his name's Paddington?"

"That's right," said Mrs Brown. "And I'm sure he didn't mean any harm."

"Harm?" The man looked at Mrs Brown in amazement. "Did you say harm? My dear lady, through the action of this bear we've had the biggest crowd in years. Our telephone hasn't stopped ringing." He waved towards the entrance to the store. "And still they come!"

He placed his hand on Paddington's head. "Barkridges," he said, "Barkridges is grateful!" He waved his other hand for silence. "We would like to show our gratitude. If there is anything… anything in the store you would like…?"

Paddington's eyes gleamed. He knew just what he wanted. He'd seen it on their way up to the outfitting department. It had been standing all by itself on a counter in the food store. The biggest one he'd ever seen. Almost as big as himself.

"Please," he said. "I'd like one of those jars of marmalade. One of the big ones."

If the manager of Barkridges felt surprised he didn't show it. He stood respectfully to one side, by the entrance to the lift.

"Marmalade it shall be," he said, pressing the button.

"I think," said Paddington, "if you don't mind, I'd rather use the stairs."

3

Trouble at the Launderette

The green front door of number thirty-two Windsor Gardens slowly opened and some whiskers and two black ears poked out through the gap. They turned first to the right, then to the left, and then suddenly disappeared from view again.

A few seconds later the quiet of the morning was broken by a strange trundling noise followed by a series of loud bumps as Paddington lowered Mr Brown's wheelbarrow down the steps and on to the pavement. He peered up and down the street once more and then hurried back indoors.

Paddington made a number of journeys back and forth between the house and the wheelbarrow and each time he came through the front door he was carrying a large pile of things in his paws.

There were clothes, sheets, pillow-cases, towels, several tablecloths, not to mention a number of old jerseys belonging to Mr Curry, all of which he carefully placed in the barrow.

Paddington was pleased there was no one about. He felt sure that neither the Browns nor Mr Curry would approve if they knew he was taking their washing to the launderette in a wheelbarrow. But an emergency had arisen and Paddington wasn't the sort of bear who allowed himself to be beaten by trifles.

One way and another, Paddington had been having a busy time. With Mrs Bird away and Mr and Mrs Brown ill in bed for the past two days, he hadn't known whether he was coming or going. To add to his troubles, the Browns' housekeeper had phoned to say she was arriving back shortly before lunch so there had been a lot of clearing up to do. He had spent most of the early part of the morning going round the house with what was left of her feather duster, getting rid of flour stains from the previous day's cooking and generally making everything neat and tidy.

It was while he had been dusting the mantelpiece in the dining-room that he'd suddenly come across a small pile of money and one of Mrs Bird's notes. Mrs Bird often left notes about the house reminding people to do certain things. This one was headed LAUNDRY and it was heavily underlined.

Not only did it say that the Browns' laundry was due to be collected that very day, but it also had a postscript on the end saying that Mr Curry had arranged to send some things as well and would they please be collected.

Paddington hurried around as fast as he could but it still took him some while to gather together all the Browns' washing, and having to fetch Mr Curry's had delayed things even more. He'd been so busy making out a list of all the things that he'd quite failed to hear the knock at the front door and had arrived there just in time to see the laundry van disappearing down the road. Paddington had run after it shouting and waving his paws but either the driver hadn't seen him, or he hadn't wanted to, for the van had turned a corner before he was even halfway down Windsor Gardens.

It was while he was sitting on the pile of washing in the hall, trying to decide what to do next and how to explain it all to Mrs Bird, that the idea of the launderette had entered Paddington's mind.

In the past, Mr Gruber had often spoken to him on the subject of launderettes. Mr Gruber took his own washing along to one every Wednesday evening when they stayed open late.

"And very good it is, too, Mr Brown," he was fond of saying. "You simply put the clothes into a big machine and then sit back while it does all the work for you. You meet some interesting people as well. I've had many a nice chat. And if you don't want to chat you can always watch the washing going round and round inside the machine."

Mr Gruber always made it sound most interesting and Paddington had often wanted to investigate the matter. The only difficulty as far as he could see was getting all the laundry there in the first place. The Browns always had a lot of washing, far too much to go into his shopping basket on wheels, and the launderette was some way away at the top of a hill.

In the end Mr Brown's wheelbarrow had seemed the only answer to the problem. But now that he had finished loading it and was about to set off, Paddington looked at it rather doubtfully. He could only just reach the handles with his paws and when he tried to lift the barrow it was much heavier than he had expected. Added to that, there was such a pile of washing on board he couldn't see round the sides let alone over the top, which made pushing most difficult.

To be on the safe side he tied a handkerchief to the end of an old broomstick which he stuck in the front of the barrow to let people know he was coming. Paddington had often seen the same thing done on lorries when they had a heavy load, and he didn't believe in taking any chances.

Quite a number of people turned to watch Paddington's progress as he made his way slowly up the long hill. Several times he got the wheel caught in a drain and had to be helped out by a kindly passer-by, and at one point, when he had to cross a busy street, a policeman held up all the traffic for him.

Paddington thanked him very much and raised his hat to all the waiting cars and buses, which tooted their horns in reply.

It was a hot day and more than once he had to stop and mop his brow with a pillow-case, so that he wasn't at all sorry when he rounded a corner and found himself outside the launderette.

He sat down on the edge of the pavement for a few minutes in order to get his breath back and when he got up again he was surprised to find a rusty old bicycle wheel lying on top of the washing.

"I expect someone thought you were a rag-and-bone bear," said the stout, motherly lady in charge of the launderette, who came outside to see what was going on.

"A rag-and-bone bear?" exclaimed Paddington hotly. He looked most offended. "I'm not a rag-and-bone bear. I'm a laundry bear."

The lady listened while Paddington explained what he had come for and at once called out for one of the other assistants to give him a hand up the steps with his barrow.

"I suppose you're doing it for the whole street?" she asked, as she viewed the mountain of washing.

"Oh, no," said Paddington, waving his paw vaguely in the direction of Windsor Gardens. "It's for Mrs Bird."

"Mrs Bird?" repeated the stout lady, looking at Mr Curry's jerseys and some old gardening socks of Mr Brown's which were lying on top of the pile. She opened her mouth as if she were about to say something but closed it again hurriedly when she saw Paddington staring at her.

"I'm afraid you'll need four machines for all this lot," she said briskly, as she went behind the counter. "It's a good job it's not one of our busy mornings. I'll put you in the ones at the end – eleven, twelve, thirteen and fourteen – then you'll be out of the way." She looked at Paddington. "You do know how to work them?"

"I think so," said Paddington, trying hard to remember all that Mr Gruber had told him.

"Well, if you get into any trouble the instructions are on the wall." The lady handed Paddington eight little plastic tubs full of powder. "Here's the soap powder," she continued, "That's two tubs for each machine. You tip one tubful in a hole in the top each time a red light comes on. That'll be four pounds, please."

Paddington counted out Mrs Bird's money and after thanking the lady began trundling his barrow along to the other end of the room.

As he steered his barrow in and out of people's feet he looked around the launderette with interest. It was exactly as Mr Gruber had described it to him. The washing machines, all white and gleaming, were in a line round the walls and in the middle of the room were two long rows of chairs. The machines had glass portholes in their doors and Paddington peered through several of them as he went past and watched the washing going round and round in a flurry of soapy water.

By the time he reached the end of the room he felt quite excited and he was looking forward to having a go with the Browns' washing.

Having climbed up on one of the chairs and examined the instructions on the wall,

Paddington tipped his laundry out on to the floor and began sorting it into four piles, putting all Mr Curry's jerseys into one machine and all the Browns' washing into the other three.

But although he had read the instructions most carefully, Paddington soon began to wish Mr Gruber was there to advise him. First of all there was the matter of a knob on the front of each machine. It was marked 'Hot Wash' and 'Warm Wash', and Paddington wasn't at all sure about it. But being a bear who believed in getting his money's worth he decided to turn them all to 'Hot'.

And then there was the question of the soap. Having four machines to look after made things very difficult, especially as he had to climb up on a chair each time in order to put it in. No sooner had a red light gone out on one machine than another lit up and Paddington spent the first ten minutes rushing between the four machines pouring soap through the holes in the top as fast as he could. There was a nasty moment when he accidentally poured some soap into number ten by mistake and all the water bubbled over the side, but the lady whose machine it was was very nice about it and explained that she'd already put two lots in. Paddington was glad when at long last all the red lights went out and he was able to sit back on one of the seats and rest his paws.

He sat there for some while watching the washing being gently tossed round and round, but it was such a nice soothing motion and he felt so tired after his labours that in no time at all he dropped off to sleep. Suddenly he was brought back to life by the sound of a commotion and by someone poking him.

It was the stout lady in charge and she was staring at one of Paddington's machines. "What have you got in number fourteen?" she demanded.

"Number fourteen?" Paddington thought for a moment and then consulted his laundry list. "I think I put some jerseys in there," he said.

The stout lady raised her hands in horror. "Oh, Else," she cried, calling to one of her assistants. "There's a young bear here put 'is jerseys in number fourteen by mistake!"

"What!" cried Paddington. "I didn't put them in by mistake – I did it on purpose. Besides," he added, looking most worried at the expression on the lady's face, "they're not my jerseys – they're Mr Curry's."

"Well, whoever they belong to," said the lady, as she hurriedly switched off the machine, "I hope he's long and thin."

"Oh dear," said Paddington, getting more and more worried. "I'm afraid Mr Curry's rather short."

"That's a pity," said the lady sympathetically, "because he's got some long, thin jerseys now. You had the machine switched to 'Hot Wash' and you should never do that with woollens. There's a special notice about that."

Paddington gazed in horror as the lady withdrew a dripping mass of wool from the machine and placed it in his barrow.

"Mr Curry's jerseys!" he said bitterly to the world in general as he sank back in his chair.

Paddington had been a bit worried about Mr Curry's jerseys right from the start. After the episode of the kitchen table★ he hadn't been very keen on meeting Mr Curry and he'd had to lie in wait until the coast was clear before slipping into his kitchen. He'd found the jerseys in a pile by the sink but there had been nothing to say whether they were meant to be washed or not. Paddington had a nasty feeling in the back of his mind that the answer was 'not', and now he was sure of it.

Paddington often found that shocks came in twos and as he sat back in his chair he received his second shock of the morning.

His eyes nearly popped out of his head as one of the other machines containing the Browns' washing began making a very strange whirring noise. The whirring was followed by several loud clicks and Paddington stared at the machine in amazement as the washing inside began to spin round faster and faster until it suddenly disappeared leaving a gaping hole in the middle.

He jumped up and peered through the porthole at the empty space where, only a few moments before, his washing had been. Then he hurriedly began to undo the knob on the side of the machine. It was all very strange and it definitely needed investigating.

Paddington wasn't quite sure what happened next, but as he opened the door a stream of hot, soapy water shot out, nearly knocking his hat off, and as he fell over backwards on the floor most of Mrs Bird's washing seemed to land on top of his head.

Paddington lay on his back in a pool of water and listened to the shrieks and cries going on all around him. Then he closed his eyes, put his paws in his ears and waited for the worst to happen.

"I think they've been having trouble up at the launderette," said Mrs Bird. "When I came past in the bus just now there was quite a crowd outside and water running out of the door – not to mention bubbles everywhere."

"The launderette?" said Mrs Brown, looking rather worried.

"That's right," said Mrs Bird. "And Mr Curry's had a burglary. Someone broke into his kitchen in broad daylight and took some jerseys he'd put out for mending."

Mrs Bird had just arrived back from her holiday and she was exchanging all the news with Mrs Brown. "If I'd known what was going on," she continued, "I wouldn't have had a minute's peace. Jonathan and Judy away and you and Mr Brown ill in bed!" She raised her hands in horror at the thought of it all.

"We've been doing very well," said Mr Brown, as he sat up in bed. "Paddington's been looking after us."

"Hmmm," said Mrs Bird. "That's as may be." Mrs Bird had made her way upstairs and she had also found the remains of her feather duster hidden in the hall-stand.

"Have you seen Paddington anywhere?" asked Mrs Brown. "He went out just now but he said he wouldn't be very long."

"No," said Mrs Bird. "And that's another thing. There are wheelbarrow trails right through the house. All the way up from the shed, through the kitchen and out through the front door."

"*Wheelbarrow* trails?" repeated Mr Brown. "But we've been in bed for two days."

"That," said Mrs Bird sternly, "is exactly what I mean!"

While the Browns were trying to solve the mystery of the wheelbarrow trails, Paddington was having an even more difficult time in the launderette.

"But I only opened the door to see where the washing had gone," he explained. He was sitting on the counter wrapped in a blanket while the mess was being cleared up.

"But it hadn't gone anywhere," said the stout lady. "The things only *looked* as if they had disappeared because they were going round so fast. They always do that." She sought for words to explain what she meant.

"It's a... it's a sort of phenomenon."

"A phen-omen-on?" repeated Paddington. "But it didn't say anything about a phenomenon in the instructions."

The lady sighed. Washing machines were rather difficult things to explain and she'd not had many dealings with bears before.

"Bubbles all over my machines!" she exclaimed. "Water all over the floor. I've never seen such a mess!"

"Oh dear," said Paddington sadly. "I'm in trouble again." He looked at the pile of half-washed clothes next to him. He didn't know what Mrs Bird would say when she heard all about it, and as for Mr Curry...

"I tell you what," said the stout lady as she caught sight of the expression on Paddington's face. "Seeing it's your first time here and we're not so very busy, suppose we do it all again. It would never do to have a dissatisfied customer in a launderette." She gave Paddington a wink. "Then we can put it all in the spin dryer and if I've got time I might even be able to iron it for you in the back room. After all, it's not every day we have a bear's washing to do."

Mrs Bird surveyed the neat pile of newly ironed laundry and then turned to Mr and Mrs Brown who had just come downstairs for the first time. "Well," she said approvingly, "I never expected to see this. I couldn't have done it better myself."

"I do hope it's all right, Mrs Bird," said Paddington anxiously. "I had a bit of a phenomenon in the launderette."

"A phenomenon?" repeated Mrs Brown. "But you can't have a phenomenon in a washing machine."

"I did," said Paddington firmly. "And all the water came out."

"I think you must be mistaken, dear," said Mrs Brown. "A phenomenon means something strange."

"And talking of strange things," said Mrs Bird, looking hard at

Paddington, "Mr Curry knocked on the door a moment ago and left you a toffee. He says he's very pleased with his jerseys. He doesn't know what you've done to them but they fit him for the first time in years. They've always been too large up till now."

"Perhaps," said Mr Brown, "there was a phenomenon in the washing machine after all."

Paddington felt very pleased with himself as he made his way upstairs to his room. He was glad it had turned out all right in the end. As he closed the dining-room door he just caught a remark of Mrs Bird's.

"I think we're very lucky indeed," she said. "Looking after a big house like this for two days and doing all the washing into the bargain. That young bear's one of the old school."

Paddington puzzled over the remark for some time and in the end he went to consult his friend Mr Gruber on the subject.

When Mr Gruber explained to him that it meant he was very reliable, Paddington felt even more pleased. Compliments from Mrs Bird were very rare.

"But all the better for having when they come, Mr Brown," said Mr Gruber. "All the better for having when they come."

4

A Spot of Decorating

Paddington gave a deep sigh and pulled his hat down over his ears in an effort to keep out the noise. There was such a hullabaloo going on it was difficult to write up the notes in his scrapbook.

The excitement had all started when Mr and Mrs Brown and Mrs Bird received an unexpected invitation to a wedding. Luckily both Jonathan and Judy were out for the day or things might have been far worse. Paddington hadn't been included in the invitation, but he didn't really mind. He didn't like weddings very much – apart from the free cake – and he'd been promised a piece of that whether he went or not.

All the same he was beginning to wish everyone would hurry up and go. He had a special reason for wanting to be alone that day.

He sighed again, wiped the pen carefully on the back of his paw, and then mopped up some ink blots which somehow or other had found their way on to the table. He was only just in time, for at that moment the door burst open and Mrs Brown rushed in.

"Ah, there you are, Paddington!" She stopped short in the middle of the room and stared at him. "Why on earth are you wearing your hat indoors?"

she asked. "And why is your tongue all blue?"

Paddington stuck out his tongue as far as he could. "It *is* a funny colour," he admitted, squinting down at it with interest. "Perhaps I'm sickening for something!"

"You'll be sickening for something all right if you don't clear up this mess," grumbled Mrs Bird as she entered. "Just look at it. Bottles of ink. Glue. Bits of paper. My best sewing scissors. Marmalade all over the table runner, and goodness knows what else."

Paddington looked around. It *was* in a bit of a state.

"I've almost finished," he announced. "I've just got to rule a few more lines and things. I've been writing my memories."

Paddington took his scrapbook very seriously and spent many long hours carefully pasting in pictures and writing up his adventures. Since he'd been at the Browns', so much had happened it was now more than half full.

"Well, make sure you *do* clear everything up," said Mrs Brown, "or we shan't bring you back any cake. Now do take care of yourself. And don't forget – when the baker comes we want two loaves." With that she waved goodbye and followed Mrs Bird out of the room.

"You know," said Mrs Bird, as she stepped into the car, "I have a feeling that bear has something up his paw. He seemed most anxious for us to leave."

"Oh, I don't know," said Mrs Brown. "I don't see what he *can* do. We shan't be away all that long."

"Ah!" replied Mrs Bird darkly. "That's as may be. But he's been hanging about on the landing upstairs half the morning. I'm sure he's up to something."

Mr Brown, who didn't like weddings much either, and was secretly wishing he could stay at home with Paddington, looked over his shoulder as he let in the clutch. "Perhaps I ought to stay as well," he said. "Then I could get on with decorating his new room."

"Now, Henry," said Mrs Brown firmly. "You're coming to the wedding and that's that. Paddington will be quite all right by himself. He's a very capable bear. And as for you wanting to get on with decorating his new room… you haven't done a thing towards it for over a fortnight, so I'm sure it can wait another day."

Paddington's new room had become a sore point in the Brown household. It was over two weeks since Mr Brown had first thought of doing it. So far he had stripped all the old wallpaper from the walls, removed the picture rails, the wood round the doors, the door handle, and everything else that was loose, or that he had made loose, and bought a lot of bright new wallpaper, some whitewash, and some paint. There matters had rested.

In the back of the car Mrs Bird pretended she hadn't heard a thing. An idea had suddenly come into her mind and she was hoping it hadn't entered Paddington's as well; but Mrs Bird knew the

workings of Paddington's mind better than most and she feared the worst. Had she but known, her fears were being realised at that very moment. Paddington was busy scratching out the words 'AT A LEWSE END' in his scrapbook and was adding, in large capital letters, the ominous ones: 'DECKERATING MY NEW ROOM!'

It was while he'd been writing 'AT A LEWSE END' in his scrapbook earlier in the day that the idea had come to him. Paddington had noticed in the past that he often got his best ideas when he was 'at a loose end'.

For a long while all his belongings had been packed away ready for the big move to his new room, and he was beginning to get impatient. Every time he wanted anything special he had to undo yards of string and brown paper.

Having underlined the words in red, Paddington cleared everything up, locked his scrapbook carefully in his suitcase, and hurried upstairs. He had several times offered to lend a paw with the decorating, but for some reason or other Mr Brown had put his foot down on the idea and hadn't even allowed him in the room while work was in progress. Paddington couldn't quite understand why. He was sure he would be very good at it.

The room in question was an old box-room which had been out of use for a number of years, and when he entered it, Paddington found it was even more interesting than he had expected.

He closed the door carefully behind him and sniffed. There was an exciting smell of paint and whitewash in the air. Not only that, but there were some steps, a trestle table, several brushes, a number of rolls of wallpaper, and a big pail of whitewash.

The room had a lovely echo as well, and he spent a long time sitting in the middle of the floor while he was stirring the paint, just listening to his new voice.

There were so many different and interesting things around that it was a job to know what to do first. Eventually Paddington decided on the painting. Choosing one of Mr Brown's best brushes, he dipped it into the pot of paint and then looked around the room for something to dab it on.

It wasn't until he had been working on the window-frame for several minutes that he began to wish he had started on something else. The brush made his arm ache, and when he tried dipping his paw in the paint pot instead and rubbing it on, more paint seemed to go on to the glass than the wooden part, so that the room became quite dark.

"Perhaps," said Paddington, waving the brush in the air and addressing the room in general, "perhaps if I do the ceiling first with the whitewash I can cover all the drips on the wall with the wallpaper."

But when Paddington started work on the whitewashing he found it was almost as hard as painting. Even by standing on tip-toe at the very top of the steps, he had a job to reach the ceiling. The bucket of whitewash was much too heavy for him to lift, so that he had to come down the steps every time in order to dip the brush in. And when he carried the brush up again, the whitewash ran down his paw and made his fur all matted.

Looking around him, Paddington began to wish he was still 'at a loose end'. Things were beginning to get in rather a mess again. He felt sure Mrs Bird would have something to say when she saw it.

It was then that he had a brainwave. Paddington was a resourceful bear and he didn't like being beaten by things. Recently he had become interested in a house which was being built nearby. He had first seen it from the window of his bedroom and since then he'd spent many hours talking to the men and watching while they hoisted their tools and cement up to the top floor by means of a rope and pulley. Once, Mr Briggs, the foreman, had even taken him up in the bucket too, and had let him lay several bricks.

Now the Browns' house was an old one and in the middle of the ceiling there was a large hook where a big lamp had once hung. Not only that, but in one corner of the room there was a thin coil of rope as well...

Paddington set to work quickly. First he tied one end of the rope to the handle of the bucket. Then he climbed up the steps and passed the other end through the hook in the ceiling. But even so, when he had climbed down again, it still took him a long time to pull the bucket anywhere near the top of the steps. It was full to the brim with whitewash and very heavy, so that he had to stop every few seconds and tie the other end of the rope to the steps for safety.

It was when he undid the rope for the last time that things started to go wrong. As Paddington closed his eyes and leaned back for the final pull he suddenly felt to his surprise as if he was floating on air. It was a most strange feeling. He reached out one foot and waved it around. There was definitely nothing there. He opened one eye and then nearly let go of the rope in astonishment as he saw the bucket of whitewash going past him on its way down.

Suddenly everything seemed to happen at once. Before he could even reach out a paw or shout for help, his head hit the ceiling and there was a clang as the bucket hit the floor.

For a few seconds Paddington clung there, kicking the air and not knowing what to do. Then there was a gurgling sound from below. Looking down, he saw to his horror that all the whitewash was running out of the bucket. He felt the rope begin to move again as the bucket got lighter, and then it shot past him again as he descended, to land with a bump in the middle of a sea of whitewash.

Even then his troubles weren't over. As he tried to regain his balance on the slippery floor, he let go of the rope, and with a rushing noise the bucket shot downwards again and landed on top of his head, completely covering him.

Paddington lay on his back in the whitewash for several minutes, trying to get his breath back and wondering what had hit him. When he did sit up and take the bucket off his head he quickly put it back on again. There was whitewash all over the floor, the paint pots had been upset into little rivers of brown and green, and Mr Brown's decorating cap was floating in one corner of the room. When Paddington saw it he felt very glad he'd left *his* hat downstairs.

One thing was certain – he was going to have a lot of explaining to do. And that was going to be even more difficult than usual, because he couldn't even explain to himself quite what had gone wrong.

It was some while later, when he was sitting on the upturned bucket thinking about things, that the idea of doing the wallpapering came to him. Paddington had a hopeful nature and he believed in looking on the bright side. If he did the wallpapering really well, the others might not even notice the mess he'd made.

Paddington was fairly confident about the wallpapering. Unknown to Mr Brown, he had often watched him in the past through a crack in the door, and it looked quite simple. All you had to do was to brush some sticky stuff on the back of the paper and then put it on the wall. The high parts weren't too difficult, even for a bear, because you could fold the paper in two and put a broom in the middle where the fold was. Then you simply pushed the broom up and down the wall in case there were any nasty wrinkles.

Paddington felt much more cheerful now he'd thought of the wallpapering. He found some paste already mixed in another bucket, which he put on top of the trestle while he unrolled the paper. It was a little difficult at first because every time he tried to unroll the paper he had to crawl along the trestle pushing it with his paws and the other end rolled up again and followed behind him. But eventually he managed to get one piece completely covered in paste.

He climbed down off the trestle, carefully avoiding the worst of the whitewash, which by now was beginning to dry in large lumps, and lifted the sheet of wallpaper on to a broom. It

was a long sheet of paper, much longer than it had seemed when he was putting the paste on, and somehow or other, as Paddington waved the broom about over his head, it began to wrap itself around him. After a struggle he managed to push his way out and headed in the general direction of a piece of wall. He stood back and surveyed the result. The paper was torn in several places, and there seemed to be a lot of paste on the outside, but Paddington felt quite pleased with himself. He decided to try another piece, then another, running backwards and forwards between the trestle and the walls as fast as his legs could carry him, in an effort to get it all finished before the Browns returned.

Some of the pieces didn't quite join, others overlapped, and on most of them were some very odd-looking patches of paste and whitewash. None of the pieces were as straight as he would have liked, but when he put his head on one side and squinted, Paddington felt the overall effect was quite nice, and he felt very pleased with himself.

It was as he was taking a final look round the room at his handiwork that he noticed something very strange. There was a window, and there was also a fireplace. But there was no longer any sign of a door. Paddington stopped squinting and his eyes grew rounder and rounder. He distinctly remembered there *had* been a door because he had come through it. He blinked at all four walls. It was difficult to see properly because the paint on the window-glass had started to dry and there was hardly any light coming through – but there most definitely wasn't a door!

"I can't understand it," said Mr Brown as he entered the dining-room. "I've looked everywhere and there's no sign of Paddington. I told you I should have stayed at home with him."

Mrs Brown looked worried. "Oh dear, I hope nothing's happened to him. It's so unlike him to go out without leaving a note."

"He's not in his room," said Judy.

"Mr Gruber hasn't seen him either," added Jonathan. "I've just been down to the market and he says he hasn't seen him since they had cocoa together this morning."

"Have *you* seen Paddington anywhere?" asked Mrs Brown as Mrs Bird entered, carrying a tray of supper things.

"I don't know about Paddington," said Mrs Bird. "I've been having enough trouble over the water pipes without missing bears. I think they've got an air lock or something. They've been banging away ever since we came in."

Mr Brown listened for a moment. "It *does* sound like water pipes," he said. "And yet… it isn't regular enough, somehow." He went outside into the hall. "It's a sort of thumping noise…"

"Crikey!" shouted Jonathan. "Listen… it's someone sending an S.O.S."

Everyone exchanged glances and then, in one voice, cried: "Paddington!"

"Mercy me," said Mrs Bird as they burst through the papered-up door. "There must have been an earthquake or something. And either that's Paddington or it's his ghost!" She pointed towards a small, white figure as it rose from an upturned bucket to greet them.

"I couldn't find the door," said Paddington, plaintively. "I think I must have papered it over when I did the decorating. It was there when I came in. I remember seeing it. So I banged on the floor with a broom handle."

"Gosh!" said Jonathan, admiringly. "What a mess!"

"You… papered… it over… when… you… did… the… decorating," repeated Mr Brown. He was a bit slow to grasp things sometimes.

"That's right," said Paddington. "I did it as a surprise." He waved a paw round the room. "I'm afraid it's in a bit of a mess, but it isn't dry yet."

While the idea was slowly sinking into Mr Brown's mind, Mrs Bird came to Paddington's rescue. "Now it's not a bit of good holding an inquest," she said. "What's done is done. And if you ask me it's a good thing too. Now perhaps we shall get some proper decorators in to do the job." With that she took hold of Paddington's paw and led him out of the room.

"As for you, young bear – you're going straight into a hot bath before all that plaster and stuff sets hard!"

Mr Brown looked after the retreating figures of Mrs Bird and Paddington and then at the long trail of white footprints and pawmarks. "Bears!" he said, bitterly.

Paddington hung about in his room for a long time after his bath and waited until the last possible minute before going downstairs to supper. He had a nasty feeling he was in disgrace. But surprisingly the word 'decorating' wasn't mentioned at all that evening.

Even more surprisingly, while he was sitting up in bed drinking his cocoa, several people came to see him and each of them gave him ten pence. It was all very mysterious, but Paddington didn't like to ask why in case they changed their minds.

It was Judy who solved the problem for him when she came in to say good night.

"I expect Mummy and Mrs Bird gave you ten pence because they don't want Daddy to do any more decorating," she explained. "He always starts things and never finishes them. And I expect Daddy gave you one because he didn't want to finish it anyway. Now they're getting a proper decorator in, so everyone's happy!"

Paddington sipped his cocoa thoughtfully. "Perhaps if I did another room I'd get another thirty pence," he said.

"Oh no, you don't," said Judy sternly. "You've done quite enough for one day. If I were you I shouldn't mention the word 'decorating' for a long time to come."

"Perhaps you're right," said Paddington sleepily, as he stretched out his paws. "But I *was* at a loose end."

5

Paddington at the Wheel

Paddington gave the man facing him one of his hardest stares ever. "I've won a bookmark?" he exclaimed hotly. "But I thought it was going to be a Rolls-Royce."

The man fingered his collar nervously. "There must be some mistake," he replied. "The lucky winner of the car has already been presented with it. And the second prize, a weekend for two in Paris, has gone to an Old Age Pensioner in Edinburgh. If you've had a letter from us, then you must be one of the ten thousand runners-up who merely receive bookmarks. I can't think why one wasn't enclosed."

"I'm one of ten thousand runners-up?" repeated Paddington, hardly able to believe his ears.

"I'm afraid so." Regaining his confidence, the man began rummaging in one of his desk drawers. "The trouble is," he said meaningly, "so many entrants to competitions don't bother to read the small print. If you care to take another look at our entry form you'll see what I mean."

Paddington took the leaflet and focused his gaze on a picture of a large, sleek, silvery-grey car. A chauffeur, standing beside one of the open doors, was flicking an imaginary speck of dust from the upholstery with one of his gloves, while across the bonnet, in large red letters, were the words ALL THIS COULD BE YOURS!

Having slept with an identical picture under his pillow at number thirty-two Windsor Gardens for several weeks, Paddington felt he knew it all by heart. He turned it over and on the back were the self-same instructions for entering the competition, together with an entry form.

"Now look inside," suggested the man.

Paddington did as he was bidden, and as he did so, his face fell. He'd been so excited by the picture of the Rolls-Royce he hadn't bothered to look any further, but as he pulled the pages apart, he found it opened into a larger sheet. On the left hand side, there was a picture of a French gendarme pointing towards a distant view of the Eiffel Tower, and on the right, under the heading TEN THOUSAND CONSOLATION PRIZES TO BE WON, there was a picture of a bookmark, followed by a lot of writing.

By the end of the page, some of the print was so small, Paddington began to wish he'd brought his opera glasses with him, but there was no escaping the fact that the bookmark had an all-too-familiar look about it. One exactly like it had arrived that very morning in the envelope containing news of his success.

"I don't think a bookmark is much consolation for not winning a Rolls-Royce!" exclaimed Paddington. "I put mine down the waste disposal. I didn't think it was a prize."

"Oh dear!" The man gave a sympathetic cluck as he riffled through a pile of papers on his desk to show that the interview was at an end. "How very unfortunate. Still, at least you've had the benefit of eating some of our sun-kissed currants." He opened one of his desk drawers again and took out a packet. "Have some more as a present," he said.

"But I don't even like currants!" exclaimed Paddington bitterly. "And I ate fifteen boxes of them!"

"*Fifteen?*" The man gazed at Paddington with new respect. "May I ask what your slogan was?"

"A currant a day," said Paddington hopefully, "keeps the doctor away."

"In that case," said the man, permitting himself a smile, "you shouldn't require any medical attention for quite a…" His voice trailed away as he caught sight of the look Paddington was giving him.

It had taken Paddington a long time to get through fifteen boxes of currants, not to mention think up a suitable slogan into the bargain. And, if the expression on his face was anything to go by, the whole thing had left him in need of more medical attention rather than less.

In fact, as he made his way back down the stairs, Paddington began to look more and more gloomy. The news that he wasn't after all the proud possessor of a gleaming new motor car was a bitter blow; one made all the worse because he hadn't even wanted it for himself - it had really been intended as a surprise for Mr Brown.

Mr Brown's present car was a bit of a sore point in the Brown household. The general feeling at number thirty-two Windsor Gardens was that it ought to have been pensioned off years ago. But Mr Brown had held on to it because it was hard to find anything large enough to convey the whole of the family, not to mention Paddington and all his belongings, when they went on their outings.

Apart from its age, it had a number of drawbacks, one of which was that instead of flashing lights, it relied on illuminated arms to indicate intended changes of direction. It was the failure of one of these arms, when Mr Brown had been turning into a main road one day, that had attracted the attention of a passing policeman who'd taken his number.

Paddington had been most upset at the time because he'd been sitting alongside Mr Brown, ready to help out with paw signals when necessary.

The magistrate had had one or two pointed things to say about drivers who relied on bears for their signals, and much to Mr Brown's disgust, he'd been ordered to retake his driving test.

It was shortly after this disastrous event that Paddington had come across a leaflet in the local supermarket announcing a competition in which the first prize was a car. And it was not just any old car, but a Rolls-Royce. Paddington felt sure that with a car as grand as a Rolls, Mr Brown couldn't possibly fail his coming test, let alone have any motoring problems ever again.

The competition was sponsored by a well-known brand of currants, and the lady in the supermarket assured Paddington that there had been nothing like it in the dried-fruit world before. When he consulted the leaflet, with the aid of his torch under the bedclothes that night, he could quite see what she meant, for it couldn't have been more simple. All that was required was a suitable slogan to do with currants, together with three packet tops to show that the entry was genuine.

But the thing which really clinched matters for Paddington was the discovery that not only was the result of the competition being announced on the same day that Mr Brown was due to take his test, but that the firm who were running it occupied a building in the very same street as the Test Centre.

Paddington was a great believer in coincidence; some of his best adventures had come about in just such a way - almost as if they had been meant to happen - and after buying some extra packets of currants in order to make doubly sure of success, he lost no time in sending off his entry.

The fact that in the end it had all come to nought was most disappointing, and as he left the building he paused in order to direct a few more hard stares in the direction of the upper floors. Then he collected his shopping basket on wheels from the car park outside and made his way slowly along the road towards the Test Centre.

He was much earlier than he had expected to be and so he wasn't too surprised to find Mr Brown's car still standing where it had been parked earlier that morning. Neither Mr Brown nor Mrs Brown were anywhere in sight, and being the sort of bear who didn't believe in wasting time, Paddington parked his shopping basket on wheels alongside it. Then he climbed into the driver's seat and switched on the radio while he awaited developments.

Like the car itself, Mr Brown's radio had seen better days. It somehow managed to make everything sound the same, rather like an old-fashioned horn gramophone, and in no time at all, Paddington found himself starting to nod off. His eyelids got heavier and heavier and soon the sound of gentle snoring added itself to the music.

Paddington had no idea how long he slept, but he was just in the middle of a very vivid dream in which he was driving down a long road, battling against a storm of currants as big as hailstones, when he awoke with a start and found to his surprise that two men were standing outside the car peering through the window at him. One of them was carrying a large clipboard to  which was attached a sheaf of very important-looking papers, and he was tapping on the glass in no uncertain manner.

Paddington hastily removed his paws from the steering wheel and opened the driver's door.

"Is your name Brown?" demanded the man with the clipboard, trying to make himself heard above the radio. "From number thirty-two Windsor Gardens?"

"That's right," said Paddington, looking most surprised.

"Hmm." The man gave him an odd look and then consulted the papers on his board. "Er… I take it you are a British subject?" he asked.

Paddington considered the matter for a moment. "Well," he said, "yes and no…"

"Yes and no?" repeated the man sharply. "You can't be yes *and* no. You must be one thing or the other."

"I *live* at number thirty-two Windsor Gardens," said Paddington firmly, "but I *come* from Darkest Peru."

"Darkest Peru? Oh!" The man began to look as if he rather wished he hadn't brought the matter up. Hastily changing the subject, he motioned with his free hand towards his companion. "I take it you won't mind if we're accompanied?" he asked. Then, lowering his voice, he gave Paddington a knowing wink. "We instructors have to be tested every now and again as well, you know. It's my turn today."

"I didn't know," said Paddington with interest. "Perhaps I could ask you some questions on the Highway Code. I've been testing the others at breakfast all this week."

The examiner glared at him. "No, you can't!" he snorted, above the sound of martial music from the radio. He looked as if he would have liked to say a good deal more, but instead he recovered himself and opened the rear door of the car for his superior to enter.

"Colonel Bogey," said the other man briefly, nodding towards the front of the car as he settled himself in the back seat.

Paddington raised his hat politely as the examiner made his way round the front of the car and climbed into the passenger seat. "Good morning, Mr Bogey," he said.

The man clucked impatiently. He was about to explain that his superior had only been giving the name of the tune on the radio, not an introduction, but he thought better of it. Instead, he reached forward for the switch. "I think we'll have the radio off for a start," he said severely. "I can't concentrate properly with that row on and I'm sure you can't eith…" He broke off and a strange look came over his face as he felt the seat. "I'm sitting on something," he cried. "Something wet and sticky!"

"Oh dear," said Paddington, looking most upset. "I expect that's my marmalade sandwiches. I put them there for my elevenses."

"Your *marmalade sandwiches*?" repeated the man as if in a dream. "They're all over my new trousers."

"Don't worry," said Paddington. He lifted up his hat and withdrew a small package. "I've got some more. I always keep some under my hat in case of an emergency."

The examiner's face seemed to go a funny colour. But before he had a chance to open his mouth, the man in the back reached over and tapped him on the shoulder. "Don't you think we ought to get cracking?" he said meaningly. "Time's getting on and we've a lot to get through."

The examiner took a deep breath as he gathered himself together. "I take it," he said, between his teeth, "you hold a current licence?"

"A *currant* licence?" It was Paddington's turn to look taken aback. He'd never heard of anyone needing a licence just to eat currants before. "I don't think Mrs Bird would let me be without one," he said, giving the man a hard stare.

The examiner wilted visibly under Paddington's gaze. "Perhaps you would like to switch the engine on?" he said hastily. "We, of the Department of Transport," he continued, in an attempt to regain his normal icy calm, "do find it easier to conduct our tests actually driving along the road."

Anxious to make amends, Paddington reached forward and pushed a nearby button with one of his paws. A grinding noise came from somewhere outside.

The man in the back seat gave a cough. "I think you'll find that's the windscreen wiper, Mr Brown," he said. "Why don't you try the button next to it? Don't worry," he continued, raising his voice as Paddington did as he was bidden and the engine suddenly roared into life, "we all get a little nervous at times like these."

"Oh, I'm not nervous," said Paddington. "It's just that they all look the same without my opera glasses."

"Er, quite!" The examiner gave a high-pitched laugh as he tried to humour his superior by joining in the spirit of things. "Perhaps," he said, "before we actually set out we could have a few questions on the Highway Code. Especially," he added meaningly, "as you say you've made such a study of it. What, for instance, do we look out for when we're driving at this time of the year?"

Paddington put on his thoughtful expression. "Strawberries?" he suggested, licking his lips.

"Strawberries?" repeated the examiner. "What do you mean – *strawberries?*"

"We often stop for strawberries at this time of year," said Paddington firmly. "Mrs Bird makes some special cream to go with them."

"I would hardly call strawberries a hazard," said the examiner petulantly.

"They are if you eat them going along," said Paddington firmly. "It's a job to know what to do with the stalks – especially if the ashtray's full."

"Good point," said the man in the back approvingly. "I must remember that one. So ought you," he added pointedly, addressing Paddington's companion.

The examiner took a deep breath. "I was thinking," he said slowly and carefully, "of sudden showers. If the weather has been dry for any length of time, a sudden shower can make the road surface very slippery."

Removing a sheet of paper covered with drawings from his clipboard, he decided to have another try. "If you were going along the highway," he said, pointing to one of the drawings, "and you saw this sign, what would it mean?"

Paddington peered at the drawing. "It looks like someone trying to open an umbrella," he replied.

The examiner drew in his breath sharply. "That sign," he said, "happens to mean there are roadworks ahead."

"Perhaps they're expecting one of your showers?" suggested Paddington helpfully. He gave the man another stare. For an examiner he didn't seem to know very much.

The man returned his gaze as if in a dream. In fact, if looks could have killed, the expression on his face suggested that Paddington's name would have been added to the list of road casualties with very little bother indeed. However, once again he was saved by an impatient movement from the back of the car.

"Perhaps we should move off now?" said a voice. "We seem to be getting nowhere very fast."

"Very good." Taking a firm grip of himself, the examiner settled back in his seat. "Go straight up this road about two hundred yards," he commanded, "then when you see a sign marked BEAR LEFT…"

"*A bear's been left?*" Paddington suddenly sat bolt upright. He wasn't at all sure what was going on and he'd been trying to decide whether to obey his next set of instructions or wait for Mr Brown to arrive back. The latest piece of information caused him to make up his mind very quickly indeed.

"I'm afraid I shall have to stand up to drive," he announced, as he clambered to his feet. "I can't see out properly if I'm sitting down, but I'll get there as quickly as I can."

"Now, look here," cried the examiner, a note of panic in his voice. "I didn't mean there was a *real* bear lying in the road. I only meant you're supposed to…" He broke off and stared at Paddington with disbelieving eyes. "What are you doing now?" he gasped, as Paddington bent down and disappeared beneath the dashboard.

"I'm putting the car into gear," gasped Paddington, as he took hold of the lever firmly with both paws. "I'm afraid it's a bit difficult with paws."

"But you can't change gear with your head under the dashboard," shrieked the examiner. "No one does that."

"Bears do," said Paddington firmly. And he gave the lever another hard tug just to show what he meant.

"Don't do it!" shouted the examiner. "Don't do it!"

"Let the clutch out!" came a voice from the back seat. "Let the clutch out!"

But if either of the men expected their cries to have any effect, they were doomed to disappointment. Once Paddington got an idea firmly fixed in his mind it was very difficult to get him to change course, let alone gear, and apart from hurriedly opening the car door to let out the clutch, he concentrated all his energies on the task in hand.

In the past he had often watched Mr Brown change gear. It was something Mr Brown prided himself on being able to do very smoothly indeed, so that really it was quite hard to know when it had actually taken place. But if Paddington hoped to emulate his example he failed miserably. As he gave the lever one final, desperate shove, there was a loud grinding noise followed almost immediately by an enormous jerk as the car leaped into the air like a frustrated stallion. The force of the movement caused Paddington to fall over on his back and, in his excitement, he grabbed hold of the nearest thing to hand.

"Look out!" shrieked the examiner.

But he was too late. As Paddington tightened his grip on the accelerator pedal the car shot forward with a roar like an express train. For a second or two it seemed to hover in mid-air, and then, with a crash which made the silence that followed all the more ominous, it came to a halt again.

Paddington clambered unsteadily to his feet and peered out through the windscreen. "Oh dear," he said, gazing round at the others. "I think we've hit a car in front."

The examiner closed his eyes. His lips were moving as if he was offering up a silent prayer.

"No," he said, slowly and distinctly. "You haven't got it quite right. *We* haven't hit anything, *you* have. And it isn't just a car, it's…"

The examiner broke off and gazed up at the driving mirror in mute despair as his eyes caught the reflection of those belonging to his superior in the back seat.

"It happens to be mine," said a grim voice from behind.

Paddington sank back into his seat as the full horror of the situation came home to him.

"Oh dear, Mr Bogey," he said unhappily. "I do hope that doesn't mean you've failed your test!"

As with Mr Brown's encounter with the police, Paddington's disaster at the Test Centre was a topic of conversation in the Brown household for many days afterwards. Opinions as to the possible outcome were sharply divided. There were those who thought he would be bound to hear something more, and others who thought the whole thing was so complicated nothing would be done about it, but none of them quite foresaw what would happen.

One evening, just as they were sitting down to their evening meal, there was an unexpected ring at the doorbell. Mrs Bird hurried off to answer it, and when she returned she was accompanied, to everyone's surprise, by Paddington's examiner.

"Please don't get up," he exclaimed, as Paddington jumped to his feet in alarm and hurried round to the far side of the table for safety.

He removed a large brown envelope from his briefcase and placed it on the table in front of Paddington's plate. "I… er… I happened to be passing so I thought I would drop this in for young Mr Brown."

"Oh dear," said Mrs Brown nervously. "It looks very official. I do hope it isn't bad news."

The man permitted himself a smile. "Nothing like that," he said. "Congratulations on passing your test," he continued, turning to Mr Brown. "I was glad to hear you were able to take it again so quickly. All's well that ends well, and I'm sure you'll be pleased to know that now my superior officer has had his bumper straightened, you'd hardly know anything had happened."

He mopped his brow with a handkerchief as the memory of it came flooding back. "It all sounded much worse than it actually was. As you know, I was being examined myself at the time, so I was under a certain amount of strain. As a matter of fact, I came through with flying colours. The chief examiner thought that in the circumstances I did extremely well. He's even recommended me for promotion."

"But whatever is it?" cried Judy, as Paddington opened the envelope and withdrew a sheet of paper with an inscription on it.

The examiner gave a cough. "It's a special test certificate," he said. "It enables the owner to drive vehicles in group S."

"Trust Paddington!" said Jonathan. "I bet he's the only one who's ever driven into the back of an examiner's car *and* still passed his test into the bargain."

Mr Brown gave the examiner a puzzled look. "Group *S*?" he repeated. "I didn't know there was such a thing."

"It's very rare." The examiner permitted himself another smile. "In fact there probably isn't another one like it in the whole world. It's for shopping baskets on wheels. I noticed young Mr Brown had one with him at the time of our… er… meeting."

"Gosh, Paddington." Judy gazed at him in relief. "What are you going to do with it?"

Paddington considered the matter for a moment. He really felt quite overwhelmed by his latest piece of good fortune. "I think," he announced at last, "I shall fix it to the front of my basket. Then if I ever have trouble at the supermarket cash desk I shall be able to show it."

"What a good idea," said the examiner, looking very pleased at the reception his gift had met. "And you'll be pleased to see that it's made out for life. That means," he added, gently but firmly, "that you need never, ever, *ever* come and see us to take your test again!"

6

Paddington and the Bonfire

It didn't happen overnight, but gradually there was a change in the weather. The leaves started to fall from the trees and it became dark very early in the evenings. Jonathan and Judy went back to school and Paddington was left on his own for much of the day.

But one morning, towards the end of October, a letter arrived with his name on the envelope. It was marked 'Urgent' and 'Strictly Personal' and it was in Jonathan's writing. Paddington didn't get many letters, only an occasional picture postcard from his Aunt Lucy in Peru, so it was all the more exciting.

In some ways it was a rather mysterious letter and Paddington couldn't make head or tail of it. In it Jonathan asked him to collect all the dry leaves he could find and sweep them into a pile ready for when he came home in a few days' time. Paddington puzzled about it for a long time, and in the end he decided to consult his friend Mr Gruber on the subject. Mr Gruber knew about most things, and even if he couldn't tell the answer to a question right away, he had a huge library of books in his antique shop and knew just where to look. He and Paddington often had a long chat about things in general over their morning cocoa, and Mr Gruber liked nothing better than to help Paddington with his problems.

"A problem shared is a problem halved, Mr Brown," he was fond of saying. "And I must say, that since you came to live in the district I've never been short of things to look up."

As soon as he had finished his breakfast, Paddington put on his scarf and duffle coat, collected the morning shopping list from Mrs Bird, and set off with his basket on wheels towards the shops in the Portobello Road.

Paddington enjoyed shopping. He was a popular bear with the street traders in the market, even though he usually struck a hard bargain. He always compared the prices on the various stalls very carefully before actually buying anything. Mrs Bird said he made the housekeeping money go twice as far as anyone else.

It was even colder outside than Paddington had expected, and when he stopped to look in a newsagent's on the way, his breath made the bottom of the window quite cloudy. Paddington was a polite bear, and when he saw the shopkeeper glaring at him through the door he carefully rubbed the steamy part with his paw in case anyone else wanted to look in. As he did so he suddenly noticed that the inside of the window had changed since he'd last passed that way.

Before, it had been full of chocolate and sweets. Now they were all gone and in their place was a very ragged-looking dummy sitting on top of a pile of logs. It held a notice in its hand which said:

REMEMBER, REMEMBER,

THE FIFTH OF NOVEMBER,

GUNPOWDER, TREASON, AND PLOT.

And underneath that was an even larger notice saying:

GET YOUR FIREWORKS HERE!

Paddington studied it all carefully for a few moments and then hurried on to Mr Gruber's, pausing only to pick up his morning supply of buns at the bakery, where he had a standing order.

Now that the cold weather had set in, Mr Gruber no longer sat on the pavement in front of his shop in the morning. Instead, he had arranged a sofa by the stove in the back of the shop. It was a cosy corner, surrounded by books, but Paddington didn't like it quite so much as being outside. For one thing, the sofa was an old one and some of the horsehairs poked through, but he quickly forgot about this as he handed Mr Gruber his share of buns and began telling him of the morning's happenings.

"Gunpowder, treason and plot?" said Mr Gruber, as he handed Paddington a large mug of steaming cocoa. "Why, that's to do with Guy Fawkes' Day."

He smiled apologetically and rubbed the steam from his glasses when he saw that Paddington still looked puzzled.

"I always forget, Mr Brown," he said, "that you come from Darkest Peru. I don't suppose you know about Guy Fawkes."

Paddington wiped the cocoa from his whiskers with the back of his paw in case it left a stain and shook his head.

"Well," continued Mr Gruber. "I expect you've seen fireworks before. I seem to remember when I was in South America many years ago they always had them on fête days."

Paddington nodded. Now that Mr Gruber mentioned it, he did remember his Aunt Lucy taking him to a firework display. Although he'd only been very small at the time he had enjoyed it very much.

"We only have fireworks once a year here," said Mr Gruber. "On November the Fifth." And then he went on to tell Paddington all about the plot to blow up the Houses of Parliament many years ago, and how its discovery at the last moment had been celebrated ever since by the burning of bonfires and letting off of fireworks.

Mr Gruber was very good at explaining things and Paddington thanked him when he had finished.

Mr Gruber sighed and a far-away look came into his eyes. "It's a long time since I had any fireworks of my own, Mr Brown," he said. "A very long time indeed."

"Well, Mr Gruber," said Paddington, importantly. "I think we're going to have a display. You must come to ours."

Mr Gruber looked so pleased at being invited that Paddington hurried off at once to finish his shopping. He was anxious to get back to the newsagent's quickly so that he could investigate the fireworks properly.

When he entered the shop the man looked at him doubtfully over the top of the counter. "Fireworks?" he said. "I'm not sure that I'm supposed to serve young bears with fireworks."

Paddington gave him a hard stare. "In Darkest Peru," he said, remembering all that Mr Gruber had told him, "we had fireworks every fête day."

"I dare say," said the man. "But this isn't Darkest Peru – nor nothing like it. What do you want – bangers or the other sort?"

"I think I'd like to try some you can hold in the paw for a start," said Paddington.

The man hesitated. "All right," he said. "I'll let you have a packet of best sparklers. But if you singe your whiskers don't come running to me grumbling and wanting your money back."

Paddington promised he would be very careful and was soon hurrying back up the road towards the Browns' house. As he rounded the last corner he bumped into a small boy wheeling a pram.

The boy held out a cap containing several coppers and touched his hat

respectfully. "Penny for the guy, sir."

"Thank you very much," said Paddington, taking a penny out of the cap. "It's very kind of you."

"Oi!" said the boy as Paddington turned to go. "Oi! You're supposed to give me a penny – not take one yourself."

Paddington stared at him. "Give *you* a penny?" he said, hardly able to believe his ears. "What for?"

"For the guy, of course," said the boy. "That's what I said – a penny for the guy!" He pointed to the pram and Paddington noticed for the first time that there was a figure inside it. It was dressed in an old suit and wearing a mask. It looked just like the one he'd seen in the shop window earlier that morning.

Paddington was so surprised that he had undone his suitcase and placed a penny in the boy's hat before he really knew what he was doing.

"If you don't like giving a penny for the guy," said the small boy as he turned to go, "why don't you get one of your own? All you need is an old suit and a bit of straw."

Paddington was very thoughtful as he made his way home. He even almost forgot to ask for a second helping at lunch.

"I do hope he hasn't hit on another of his ideas," said Mrs Brown, as Paddington asked to be excused and disappeared into the garden. "It's most unlike him to have to be reminded about things like that. Especially when it's stew. He's usually so fond of dumplings."

"I expect it's an Idea," said Mrs Bird, ominously. "I know the signs."

"Well, I expect the fresh air will do him good," said Mrs Brown, looking out of the window. "And it's very good of him to offer to sweep up all the leaves. The garden's in such a mess."

"It's November," said Mrs Bird. "Guy Fawkes!"

"Oh!" said Mrs Brown. "*Oh dear!*"

For the next hour Paddington enjoyed himself in the garden with Mrs Bird's dustpan and brush. The Browns had a number of trees and very soon he had a large pile of leaves, almost twice his own height, in the middle of the cabbage patch. It was while he was sitting down for a rest in the middle of the flower bed that he felt someone watching him.

He looked up to see Mr Curry, the Browns' next-door neighbour, eyeing him suspiciously over the fence. Mr Curry wasn't very fond of bears and he was always trying to catch Paddington doing something he shouldn't so that he could report him. He had a reputation in the neighbourhood for being mean and disagreeable, and the Browns had as little to do with him as possible.

"What are you doing, bear?" he growled at Paddington. "I hope you're not thinking of setting light to all those leaves."

"Oh, no," said Paddington. "It's for Guy Fawkes."

"Fireworks!" said Mr Curry, grumpily. "Nasty things. Banging away and frightening people."

Paddington, who had been toying with the idea of trying out one of his sparklers, hastily hid the packet behind his back. "Aren't you having any fireworks then, Mr Curry?" he asked, politely.

"Fireworks?" Mr Curry looked at Paddington with distaste. "Me? I can't afford them, bear. Waste of money. And what's more, if I get any coming over in my garden I shall report the whole matter to the police!"

Paddington felt very glad he hadn't tested his sparkler.

"Mind you, bear" – a sly gleam came into Mr Curry's eye and he looked around carefully to make sure no one else was listening – "if anyone likes to invite me to their firework display, that's a different matter." He signalled

Paddington over to the fence and began whispering in his ear. As Paddington listened his face got longer and longer and his whiskers began to sag.

"I think it's disgraceful," said Mrs Bird later on that day when she heard that Mr Curry had invited himself to the firework party. "Frightening a young bear like that with talk of police and such like. Just because he's too mean to buy his own fireworks. It's a good job he didn't say it to me – I'd have told him a thing or two!"

"Poor Paddington," said Mrs Brown. "He looked most upset. Where is he now?"

"I don't know," said Mrs Bird. "He's gone off somewhere looking for some straw. I expect it's to do with his bonfire."

She returned to the subject of Mr Curry. "When I think of all the errands that young bear's run for him – wearing his paws to the bone – just because he's too lazy to go himself."

"He does take advantage of people," said Mrs Brown. "Why, he even left his old suit on the porch this morning to be collected by our laundry for cleaning."

"Did he?" exclaimed Mrs Bird, grimly. "Well, we'll soon see about *that*!" She hurried out to the front door and then called out to Mrs Brown. "You *did* say the porch?"

"That's right," replied Mrs Brown. "In the corner."

"It's not there now," called Mrs Bird. "Someone must have taken it away."

"That's very strange," said Mrs Brown. "I didn't hear anyone knock. And the laundryman hasn't been yet. How very odd."

"It'll serve him right," said Mrs Bird, as she returned to the kitchen, "if someone's taken it. That'll teach him a lesson!" In spite of her stern appearance, Mrs Bird was a kindly soul at heart, but she became very cross when people took advantage of others, especially Paddington.

"Oh well," said Mrs Brown. "I expect it'll sort itself out. I must try and remember to ask Paddington if he's seen it when he comes in."

As it happened Paddington was gone for quite a long time, so that when he did finally return, Mrs Brown had forgotten all about the matter. It had been dark for some time when he let himself into the garden by the back way. He pushed his basket up the path until he reached Mr Brown's shed, and then, after a struggle, managed to lift a large object out of the basket, and place it in a corner behind the lawn-mower. There was also a small cardboard box marked GI FAWKES, which rattled when he shook it.

Paddington shut the door of the shed, carefully hid the cardboard box underneath his hat in the bottom of the basket, and then crept quietly out of the garden and round to the front door. He felt pleased with himself. It had been a very good evening's work indeed – much better than he had expected – and that night, before he went to sleep, he spent a long time writing a letter to Jonathan in which he told him all about it.

"Gosh, Paddington," exclaimed Jonathan, several days later, when they were getting ready for the display. "What a super lot of fireworks!" He peered into the cardboard box, which was full almost to the brim. "I've never seen so many."

"Honestly, Paddington," said Judy admiringly. "Anyone would think you'd been collecting in the street or something."

Paddington waved a paw vaguely through the air and exchanged a knowing glance with Jonathan. But before he had time to explain things to Judy, Mr Brown entered the room.

He was dressed in an overcoat and gumboots and he was carrying a lighted candle. "Right," he said. "Are we all ready? Mr Gruber's waiting in the hall and

Mrs Bird's got the chairs all ready on the veranda." Mr Brown looked as eager as anyone to start the firework display and he eyed Paddington's box enviously.

"I vote," he said, holding up his hand for silence when they were all outside in the garden, "that as this is Paddington's first November the Fifth, we let him set off the first firework."

"Hear! Hear!" applauded Mr Gruber. "What sort would you like, Mr Brown?"

Paddington looked thoughtfully at the box. There were so many different shapes and sizes it was difficult to decide. "I think I'll have one of those you can hold in the paw first," he said. "I think I'll have a sparkler."

"Dull things, sparklers," said Mr Curry, who was sitting in the best chair helping himself to some marmalade sandwiches.

"If Paddington wants a sparkler, he shall have one," said Mrs Bird, giving Mr Curry a freezing look.

Mr Brown handed Paddington the candle, taking care not to let the hot wax drip on to his fur, and there was a round of applause as the sparkler burst into life. Paddington waved it over his head several times and there was another round of applause as he moved it up and down to spell out the letters P–A–D–I–N–G–T–U–N.

"Very effective," said Mr Gruber.

"But that's not how you spell *Paddington*," grumbled Mr Curry, his mouth full of sandwich.

"It's how *I* spell it," said Paddington. He gave Mr Curry one of his special hard stares, but unfortunately it was dark and so the full effect was lost.

"How about lighting the bonfire?" said Mr Brown hurriedly. "Then we can all see what we're doing." There was a crackle from the dried leaves as he bent down to apply the match.

"That's better," said Mr Curry, rubbing his hands together. "I find it rather draughty on this veranda of yours. I think I'll let off a few more fireworks if there are no more sandwiches left." He looked across at Mrs Bird.

"There aren't," said Mrs Bird. "You've just had the last one. Honestly," she continued, as Mr Curry moved away and began rummaging in Paddington's box, "the cheek of some people. And he never even brought so much as a Catherine wheel himself."

"He does spoil things," said Mrs Brown. "Everyone's been looking forward to this evening. I've a good mind…" Whatever Mrs Brown had been about to say was lost as there came a cry from the direction of the garden shed.

"Crikey, Paddington," shouted Jonathan. "Why ever didn't you tell us?"

"Tell us what?" asked Mr Brown, trying to divide his attention between a Roman candle which had just fizzled out and the mysterious object which Jonathan was dragging from the shed.

"It's a guy!" shouted Judy with delight.

"It's a super one too!" exclaimed Jonathan. "It looks just like a real person. Is it yours, Paddington?"

"Well," said Paddington, "yes… and no." He looked rather worried. In the excitement he had quite forgotten about the guy which he'd used when he'd collected the money for fireworks. He wasn't at all sure he wanted the others to know about it in case too many questions were asked.

"A guy!" said Mr Curry. "Then it had better go on the bonfire." He peered at it through the smoke. For some odd reason there was a familiar look about it which he couldn't quite place.

"Oh, no," said Paddington hurriedly. "I don't think you'd better do that. It's not really for burning."

"Nonsense, bear," said Mr Curry. "I can see you don't know much about Guy Fawkes' Night. Guys are always burned." He pushed the others on one side and with the help of Mr Brown's garden rake placed the guy on top of the bonfire.

"There!" he exclaimed, as he stood back rubbing his hands. "That's better. That's what I call a bonfire."

Mr Brown removed his glasses, polished them, and then looked hard at the bonfire. He didn't recognise the suit the guy was wearing and he was glad to see it wasn't one of his. All the same, he had a nasty feeling at the back of his mind. "It... it seems a very well-dressed sort of guy," he remarked.

Mr Curry started and then stepped forward to take a closer look. Now that the bonfire was well and truly alight it was easier to see. The trousers were blazing merrily and the jacket had just started to smoulder. His eyes nearly popped out and he pointed a trembling finger towards the flames.

"That's my suit!" he roared. "My suit! The one you were supposed to send to the cleaners!"

"What!" exclaimed Mr Brown. Everyone turned to look at Paddington.

Paddington was as surprised as the others. It was the first he had heard of Mr Curry's suit. "I found it on the doorstep," he said. "I thought it had been put out for the rummage sale..."

"The *rummage sale*?" cried Mr Curry, almost beside himself with rage. "The *rummage sale*? My best suit! I'll... I'll..." Mr Curry was spluttering so much he couldn't think of anything to say. But Mrs Bird could.

"To start with," she said, "it wasn't your best suit. It's been sent to the cleaners at least six times to my knowledge. And I'm quite sure Paddington didn't know it was yours. In any case," she finished triumphantly, "who was it insisted it should go on the bonfire in the first place?"

Mr Brown tried hard not to laugh, and then he caught Mr Gruber's eye looking at him over the top of his handkerchief. "You *did*, you know," he spluttered. "You said put it on the bonfire. And Paddington tried to stop you!"

Mr Curry struggled hard for a moment as he looked from one to the other. But he knew when he was beaten. He gave one final glare all round the party and then stalked off into the night. A moment later the sound of a front door being slammed echoed round the houses.

"Well," chuckled Mr Gruber, "I must say that when young Mr Brown's around there's never a dull moment!" He felt underneath his chair and brought out a cardboard box. "Now I vote we get on with the display. And just in case we run out of fireworks – I've brought a few more along."

"You know, it's funny you should say that," said Mr Brown, feeling under *his* chair. "But I have some as well!"

Afterwards everyone in the neighbourhood voted it was the best firework display they had seen for many a year. Quite a number of people turned up to watch, and even Mr Curry was seen peeping from behind his curtains on several occasions.

And as Paddington lifted a tired paw and waved the last sparkler in the air to spell out the words T-H-E E-N-D, everyone agreed they had never seen such a successful bonfire before – or such a well-dressed guy.

7

Too Much Off the Top

One day, Paddington arrived in the Portobello Road armed with his usual supply of morning buns to find his friend, Mr Gruber, already standing outside his shop waiting for him.

"I've been looking forward to my elevenses, Mr Brown," he said, as they settled themselves down in some deckchairs on the pavement. "I haven't been quite so busy for a long time."

Mr Gruber went on to explain that English antiques of almost any shape or form were very popular in the United States and that apart from the tourists, some dealers came over simply to buy up as many as possible.

He waved his hand at all the gleaming copper pots and pans, vases, books, ornaments, and other bric-a-brac which lined the walls of his shop and overflowed out on the pavement.

"I must say I've missed your help, Mr Brown," he said. "Apart from the pleasure of our little chats, one young bear with a knowledge of antiques and an eye for a bargain is worth his weight in gold."

Mr Gruber disappeared into his shop for a moment and when he returned he was carrying an old vase. "What would you say this is, Mr

Brown?" he asked casually, holding it up to the light.

Paddington looked most surprised at such a simple question. "That's an early Spode, Mr Gruber," he replied promptly.

Mr Gruber nodded his approval. "Exactly," he said. "But you'd be surprised how many people wouldn't realise it. Do you know, Mr Brown, one young man I had working here while you were away actually called it a jug and he was going to let it go for fifty pence simply because it had this piece missing. I only just rescued it in time."

Mr Gruber fell silent as he fitted the broken piece of china back into the vase and Paddington nearly fell off his deckchair with surprise at the thought of there being people in the world who didn't know about antique pottery and how valuable it could be. "Fifty pence for a Spode!" he exclaimed, hardly able to believe his ears.

"Mind you," said Mr Gruber, "let's be fair. Not everyone has your advantage, Mr Brown. After all, you've spent so much time in this shop I believe you know almost as much about it as I do. If you ever decide to go into business, a lot of people will have to look to their laurels."

Paddington looked pleased at his friend's remarks. Mr Gruber wasn't in the habit of paying idle compliments and praise from him was praise indeed.

"Perhaps I could help by repairing that vase for you, Mr Gruber," he offered.

Mr Gruber looked at him doubtfully over the top of his glasses. Although he had a high regard for Paddington and had meant every word he'd said, he also knew that accidents could happen in the best-regulated circles, especially bears' circles. However, he was a kindly man at heart and after a moment's thought he nodded his agreement.

"It's very kind of you, Mr Brown," he said. "I know you'll take great care of it, but don't forget – 'there's many a slip 'twixt cup and lip'."

"I won't, Mr Gruber," said Paddington, as he took the vase and its broken piece and laid it carefully amongst some cabbages in the bottom of his shopping basket on wheels.

After Mr Gruber had sorted out some money for a tube of glue from a nearby stationer's, Paddington waved goodbye and hurried off up the road with a thoughtful expression on his face.

Mr Gruber's chance remark about going into business had suddenly reminded him of a notice which he'd seen in a shop window that very morning.

At the time he hadn't given it a great deal of attention, but now, as he reached the shop and stood looking at it again, he began to look more and more interested.

The shop, which was surmounted by a long striped pole, had the words S. SLOOP - GENTS HAIRDRESSING emblazoned across the door and the notice in the window said, quite simply, WILLING JUNIOR WANTED - URGENTLY.

Underneath, in rough capitals, Mr Sloop had added the information that a good wage would be paid to any keen young lad willing to learn the trade.

Paddington stood for quite some while breathing heavily on the glass until he suddenly became aware of a face on the other side watching him with equal interest.

Taking his courage in both paws, Paddington pushed open the door of the shop, dragging his shopping basket after him, and raised his hat as he bade the owner good morning.

"Morning," replied Mr Sloop

breezily, reaching for a white cloth. "What can I do for you? Short, back and sides, or would you like one of our 'all-in specials'? Haircut, shampoo and set - all for a pound. Tell you what - seeing trade's a bit slack this morning - I'll give you special bear rates - you can have the lot for seventy-five pence."

Paddington stepped back hastily as Mr Sloop waved a pair of clippers dangerously close to his head. "I haven't come for a haircut," he explained, placing his hat firmly over his ears. "I've come about the job."

"You've what?" Mr Sloop lost some of his breeziness as he stared at Paddington.

"It says in the window you want a willing junior," said Paddington hopefully.

"Blimey!" Mr Sloop stood back and examined Paddington. "You wouldn't be a very good advertisement, I must say. This is a barber's shop, not an art school. I'd have to whip all them whiskers off, for a start."

"Whip my whiskers off!" exclaimed Paddington hotly. "But I've always had them."

Mr Sloop considered the matter for a moment. "I suppose I could stand you in the window like one of them 'before and after' advertisements," he said grudgingly. "Not that I'm saying 'yes', mind. But I don't mind admitting I've been let down badly by the Job Centre. Nobody wants to sweep up hairs these days."

"Bears are good at sweeping," said Paddington eagerly. "I don't think I've done any hairs before but I often help Mrs Bird in the mornings."

"Errands," said Mr Sloop. "There'll be lots of errands to run. And you'll have to look after things when I pop out for me morning coffee. Keep the customers happy till I get back. Then there's the shop to keep clean. It's not so bad in the week - it's Saturday mornings. The steam fair rises off me scissors on a Saturday morning."

Mr Sloop mopped his brow at the thought as he gave Paddington a sidelong glance. "Some people might consider it a lot of work for… er… five pounds a week."

"Five pounds!" exclaimed Paddington, nearly falling over backwards at the thought of so much money. "Every week. That's over forty buns!"

"Done, then," said Mr Sloop, hurriedly coming to a decision before Paddington could change his mind.

"Mind you," he added, "it's only a trial. And no reading comics on the sly when me back's turned. But if you watch points and don't get up to any tricks, I might even let you have a go with the clippers in a week or so."

"Thank you very much, Mr Sloop," said Paddington gratefully. In the past he had often peered through the barber shop window and watched Mr Sloop run his clippers round the necks of his customers and the thought of actually being allowed to have a go filled him with excitement.

Mr Sloop clapped his hands together briskly and licked his lips. "No time like the present," he said. "I could do with a coffee right now. May as well take advantage of the lull, as you might say. You'll find a broom in that cupboard over there. When you've done the floor you can give the basins a going over - only mind them razors - don't go nicking yer paws. I don't want no bear's blood all over the place - it'll give the shop a bad name."

Having finished his instructions, Mr Sloop added that he wouldn't be long and then disappeared out of the door leaving Paddington standing in the middle of the shop with a slightly bemused expression on his face.

Cutting hair seemed much more complicated than it looked at first sight, and Mr Sloop's shop, though it was only small, appeared to have almost as many things inside it as a supermarket.

Along one wall was a row of several benches for customers, together with a pile of newspapers for them to read while they were waiting, and pinned to the wall behind them were a number of pictures cut from magazines showing the various styles it was possible to have.

The back of the shop was given over to a large cupboard and a number of notices. Mr Sloop didn't appear to have a great deal of trust in his fellow human beings for most of them were to do with payment and the fact that under no circumstances would any cheques be cashed or credit given.

But it was the business side of the room, where the chair itself stood, that aroused Paddington's immediate interest. Almost the whole of the wall was taken up by a long mirror and on a shelf in front of the mirror stood row upon row of bottles. There were bottles of hair oil, shampoo, setting lotion, hair restorer, cream... the list was endless and Paddington spent several minutes unscrewing caps in order to sniff the contents of the various bottles.

It wasn't until he was having a practice snip with a pair of scissors and narrowly missed cutting off one of his own whiskers that Paddington suddenly came back to earth with a bump and realised that he hadn't even started work. He hurried across to the cupboard and opened the door only to be met by a positive deluge of old brooms and brushes, not to mention white coats, towels and various other items.

As far as he could see, Mr Sloop must have been without any help in his shop for some while, for most of the things were so tangled together it took him all his time to find out which handle belonged to which broom let alone decide on the one to use.

It was when the confusion was at its height that Paddington vaguely heard a bell ringing and from his position in the back of the cupboard he suddenly realised that someone in the shop was carrying on a conversation.

"Say, do I get any service in this place?" called a voice with a strong American accent from the direction of Mr Sloop's chair.

Paddington scrambled out of the cupboard and peered across the room to where the owner of the voice lay waiting with his arms folded and his eyes closed.

"I'd like a trim, please," announced the man as he heard the commotion going on behind him. "Not too little - not too much - and don't touch the top. Make it snappy. I have a plane to catch later on and I have a lot of packing to do. Look," continued the voice impatiently, as Paddington hurried across the shop and peered hopefully out through the open door in search of Mr Sloop, "this is a barber's shop, isn't it? Do I get my hair cut or don't I? All I want is to get back to my hotel so as I can catch up on some sleep before I catch my plane. I'm that tired. I've been on my feet for a week, now…"

The man's voice trailed away into a loud yawn and to Paddington's astonishment, as he turned back into the shop he was greeted, not by a string of further complaints as he'd expected, but by a long, gentle snore.

Paddington had seen some people go to sleep quickly before, Mr Brown in particular on a Sunday afternoon was often very quick, but he'd never seen it happen quite so suddenly. He stood in the middle of the shop for a moment, looking anxiously at the figure in Mr Sloop's chair and then gradually the expression on his face was replaced by one of interest.

Although the man in the chair had obviously dozed off for the moment he'd certainly been in a great hurry. In fact, he'd definitely said to make it snappy. And although Mr Sloop hadn't actually said he could cut anyone's hair that very day he had mentioned something about having a go at a later date and he'd also said that one of Paddington's first jobs would be to keep the customers happy.

After giving the matter several moments' more thought, Paddington came to a decision. Taking care not to disturb the sleeping figure, he draped a white cloth round the man's shoulders and then picked up Mr Sloop's electric clippers which were hanging from a nearby hook.

After giving a few practice waves through the air in order to get used to the tickling sensation they made when they were switched on, Paddington applied the business end carefully to the back of the man's neck, making a wide sweeping movement with his paw as he'd often seen Mr Sloop do in the past.

The first stroke was rather disappointing. It went much deeper than he had intended and left a long white path up the back of the neck. The second stroke, on the other hand, didn't go nearly as deep so that he had to spend several minutes trying to match the two, and he cast some anxious glances over his shoulder in case Mr Sloop returned before he could repair the damage.

In fact, for the next minute or so, Paddington spent almost as much time looking out of the window as he did looking at the job in hand. When he did finally give his undivided attention to the figure in the chair, his eyes nearly popped out of their sockets with astonishment.

The clippers dropped from his paw and he stood rooted to the spot as he stared at the top of the man's head. Before he'd started work it had been covered by a mass of thick, black hair, whereas now, apart from a fringe round the ears and neck, it was almost completely bald.

The strange thing was, it must all have happened in the blink of an eyelid for quite definitely the hair had been there when he'd looked a second before.

It was all most mysterious and Paddington sat down on his suitcase with a mournful expression on his face while he considered the matter. He was beginning to regret not having asked for his wages in advance, for the more he thought about things, the more difficult it became to picture Mr Sloop paying for one day's work, let alone a week's.

It was while he was sitting on his suitcase that he suddenly caught sight of a bottle on a shelf above his head. It was a large bottle and it had a picture on the outside which showed a group of men, all with a luxuriant growth of jet black hair. But it wasn't so much the picture which caught his eye as the words underneath, which said in large red letters: DR SPOONER'S QUICK ACTION MAGIC HAIR RESTORER.

Paddington was a hopeful bear in many ways but after using up several spoons of the thick yellow liquid, even he began to admit to himself that he might be asking a little too much of Dr Spooner's tonic. Looking through his binoculars didn't help matters either for the top of the man's head remained as shiny and hairless as ever.

He was just toying desperately with the idea of buying some quick-drying black paint from a nearby hardware store in order to cover up the worst of the damage when his eye alighted on his shopping basket on wheels which was standing in a corner of the shop, and an excited gleam came into his eyes.

Carefully lifting out Mr Gruber's vase, which he placed on a shelf in front of the chair for safety, Paddington rummaged around in the basket until he found what he was looking for.

Although Mr Gruber had asked him to buy the glue for the express purpose of mending the vase, Paddington felt sure he wouldn't mind if it was used for something else in an emergency, and as far as he could see this was definitely one of the worst encounters he had ever encountered.

For the next few minutes, Paddington was very busy. Having squeezed drops of Mr Gruber's glue all over the man's head, he then rummaged around on the floor in search of some hair to fill in the vacant spot. Fortunately, being short of an assistant, Mr Sloop hadn't bothered to sweep up that morning and so there was quite a selection to choose from.

At long last Paddington stood back, and examined his handiwork with interest. All in all, he felt quite pleased with himself. Admittedly the top of the man's head had undergone a somewhat drastic change since he'd first sat in the chair - for one thing, there were now quite a number of ginger curls, not to mention blonde streaks, in the long straight black bits - and several of them were sticking out at rather an odd angle - but at least it was all covered, and he heaved a sigh of relief as he wiped his paws on the cloth in front of him.

It was as he was pushing a particularly springy ginger curl into place with his paw as a final touch that, to his alarm, the figure in the chair began to stir.

Paddington hurried round the other side of the chair and stood between Mr Sloop's customer and the mirror.

"That'll be two pounds fifty, please," he said, holding out his paw hopefully in a business-like manner as he consulted the price list on the wall.

If the man looked surprised at the sight of Paddington's paw under his nose, it was nothing compared with the expression which came over his face a moment later as he caught sight of his reflection in a mirror.

Jumping out of the chair, he pushed Paddington to one side and stood for a moment staring at the sight which met his eyes. For a second or two he seemed speechless and then he let out a roar of rage as he made a grab for the nearest object to hand.

Paddington's own look of alarm changed to one of horror as the man picked up the vase from the shelf and made as if to dash it to the ground.

"Look out!" he cried anxiously. "That's Mr Gruber's Spode."

To Paddington's surprise, his words had a far greater effect than he'd expected, for the man suddenly froze in mid-air, lowered his arms and then stared at the object in front of him with a look of disbelief.

"Thank you very much," said Paddington gratefully as he withdrew the vase from the man's hands and placed it carefully in his shopping basket on wheels. "It's got a piece missing already and I don't think Mr Gruber would like it very much if the rest was broken. Perhaps you'd like to break one of Mr Sloop's bottles instead," he added generously. "He's got some old ones in the cupboard."

The man took a deep breath, looked at himself once again in the mirror, passed a trembling hand over his brow and then turned back to Paddington.

"Now see here, bear," he said. "I don't know what's been going on. Maybe it's all part of a bad dream; maybe I'm going to wake up in a minute – but this Mr Gruber, he's a friend of yours?"

"He's my special friend," said Paddington importantly. "We have buns and cocoa together every morning."

"And this is the Spode?" asked the man.

"Yes," said Paddington in surprise. "He's got lots. He keeps an antique shop and…"

"Lead me to him, bear," said the man warmly. "Just lead me to him."

Mr Gruber took one last look out of his door to make sure everything was in for the night and then turned back to Paddington.

"You know, Mr Brown," he said, as they settled themselves on the horsehair sofa at the back of the shop, "I still can't believe it. I really can't."

Paddington, nodding from behind a cloud of cocoa steam, looked very much as if he agreed with every word.

"If anyone mentions the word 'coincidence' to me again," continued Mr Gruber, "I shall always tell them the story of the day you got a job as a hairdresser and knocked the toupee off an American antique dealer's head."

"I thought I'd cut all his hair off by mistake, Mr Gruber," admitted Paddington.

Mr Gruber chuckled at the thought. "I shouldn't like to have been in your paws if you really had, Mr Brown. Fancy," he continued, "if you hadn't knocked his toupee off and put all that glue on his head he wouldn't have got cross. And if you hadn't put my Spode on the shelf he wouldn't have heard about my shop. And if he hadn't heard about my shop he would have gone back to America tonight without half the things he came over to buy. It's what they call a chain of events, Mr Brown, and a very good day's work into the bargain. I can see I shall have to go to a few more sales to make up for all those empty spaces on my shelves."

Paddington looked out through the window and then sniffed the warm air from the stove. Most of the other shops in the Portobello Road already had their shutters up, and even those that were still open showed signs of closing for the night as one by one their lights went out.

"And if all those things hadn't happened, Mr Gruber," he said, as he reached across for the earthenware jug, "we shouldn't be sitting here now."

Paddington always enjoyed his cups of cocoa with Mr Gruber, but it was most unusual to have one together so late in the day and he was anxious to make the most of it.

Mr Gruber nodded his head in agreement. "And that, if I may say so, Mr Brown," he said warmly, "is the nicest link of all."

8

Christmas

Paddington found that Christmas took a long time to come. Each morning when he hurried downstairs he crossed the date off the calendar, but the more days he crossed off the farther away it seemed.

However, there was plenty to occupy his mind. For one thing, the postman started arriving later and later in the morning, and when he did finally reach the Browns' house there were so many letters to deliver he had a job to push them all through the letter-box. Often there were mysterious-looking parcels as well, which Mrs Bird promptly hid before Paddington had time to squeeze them.

A surprising number of the envelopes were addressed to Paddington himself, and he carefully made a list of all those who had sent him Christmas cards so that he could be sure of thanking them.

"You may be only a small bear," said Mrs Bird, as she helped him arrange the cards on the mantelpiece, "but you certainly leave your mark."

Paddington wasn't sure how to take this, especially as Mrs Bird had just polished the hall floor, but when he examined his paws they were quite clean.

Paddington had made his own Christmas cards. Some he had drawn himself, decorating the edges with holly and mistletoe; others had been made out of pictures cut from Mrs Brown's magazines. But each one had the words A MERRY CHRISTMAS AND A HAPPY NEW YEAR printed on the front, and they were signed PADINGTUN BROWN on the inside – together with his special paw mark to show that they were genuine.

Paddington wasn't sure about the spelling of A MERRY CHRISTMAS. It didn't look at all right. But Mrs Bird checked all the words in a dictionary for him to make certain.

"I don't suppose many people get Christmas cards from a bear," she explained. "They'll probably want to keep them, so you ought to make sure they are right."

One evening Mr Brown arrived home with a huge Christmas tree tied to the roof of his car. It was placed in a position of honour by the dining-room window and both Paddington and Mr Brown spent a long time decorating it with coloured electric lights and silver tinsel.

Apart from the Christmas tree, there were paper chains and holly to be put up, and large coloured bells made of crinkly paper. Paddington enjoyed doing the paper chains. He managed to persuade Mr Brown that bears were very good at putting up decorations and together they did most of the house, with Paddington standing on Mr Brown's shoulders while Mr Brown handed up the drawing pins. It came to an unhappy end one evening when Paddington accidentally put his paw on a drawing pin which he'd left on top of Mr Brown's head. When Mrs Bird rushed into the dining-room to see what all the fuss was about, and to inquire why all the lights had suddenly gone out, she found Paddington hanging by his paws from the chandelier and Mr Brown dancing around the room rubbing his head.

But by then the decorations were almost finished and the house had taken on quite a festive air. The sideboard was groaning under the weight of nuts and oranges, dates and figs, none of which Paddington was allowed to touch, and Mr Brown had stopped smoking his pipe and was filling the air instead with the smell of cigars.

The excitement in the Browns' house mounted, until it reached fever pitch a few days before Christmas, when Jonathan and Judy arrived home for the holidays.

But if the days leading up to Christmas were busy and exciting, they were nothing compared with Christmas Day itself.

The Browns were up early on Christmas morning – much earlier than they had intended. It all started when Paddington woke to find a large pillow-case at the bottom of his bed. His eyes nearly popped out with astonishment when he switched his torch on, for it was bulging with parcels, and it certainly hadn't been there when he'd gone to bed on Christmas Eve.

Paddington's eyes grew larger and larger as he unwrapped the brightly coloured paper round each present. A few days before, on Mrs Bird's instructions, he had made a list of all the things he hoped to have given him and had hidden it up one of the chimneys. It was a strange thing, but everything on that list seemed to be in the pillow-case.

There was a large chemistry outfit from Mr Brown, full of jars and bottles and test tubes, which looked very interesting. And there was a miniature xylophone from Mrs Brown, which pleased him no end. Paddington was fond of music – especially the loud sort, which was good for conducting – and he had always wanted something he could actually play.

Mrs Bird's parcel was even more exciting, for it contained a checked cap which he'd specially asked for and had underlined on his list. Paddington stood on the end of his bed, admiring the effect in the mirror for quite a while.

Jonathan and Judy had each given him a travel book. Paddington was very interested in geography, being a much-travelled bear, and he was pleased to see there were plenty of maps and coloured pictures inside.

The noise from Paddington's room was soon sufficient to wake both

Jonathan and Judy, and in no time at all the whole house was in an uproar, with wrapping paper and bits of string everywhere.

"I'm as patriotic as the next man," grumbled Mr Brown. "But I draw the line when bears start playing the National Anthem at six o'clock in the morning – especially on a xylophone."

As always, it was left to Mrs Bird to restore order. "No more presents until after lunch," she said firmly. She had just tripped over Paddington on the upstairs landing, where he was investigating his new chemical outfit, and something nasty had gone in one of her slippers.

"It's all right, Mrs Bird," said Paddington, consulting his instruction book, "it's only some iron filings. I don't think they're dangerous."

"Dangerous or not," said Mrs Bird, "I've a big dinner to cook – not to mention your birthday cake to finish decorating."

Being a bear, Paddington had two birthdays each year – one in the summer and one at Christmas – and the Browns were holding a party in his honour to which Mr Gruber had been invited.

After they'd had breakfast and been to church, the morning passed quickly and Paddington spent most of his time trying to decide what to do next. With so many things from which to choose it was most difficult. He read some chapters from his books and made several interesting smells and a small explosion with his chemical outfit.

Mr Brown was already in trouble for having given it to him, especially when Paddington found a chapter in the instruction book headed 'Indoor Fireworks'. He made himself a 'never ending' snake which wouldn't stop growing and frightened Mrs Bird to death when she met it coming down the stairs.

"If we don't watch out," she confided to Mrs Brown, "we shan't last over Christmas. We shall either be blown to smithereens or poisoned. He was testing my gravy with some litmus paper just now."

Mrs Brown sighed. "It's a good job Christmas only comes once a year," she said as she helped Mrs Bird with the potatoes.

"It isn't over yet," warned Mrs Bird.

Fortunately, Mr Gruber arrived at that moment and some measure of order was established before they all sat down to dinner.

Paddington's eyes glistened as he surveyed the table. He didn't agree with Mr Brown when he said it all looked too good to eat. All the same, even Paddington got noticeably slower towards the end when Mrs Bird brought in the Christmas pudding.

"Well," said Mr Gruber, a few minutes later, as he sat back and surveyed his empty plate, "I must say that's the best Christmas dinner I've had for many a day. Thank you very much indeed!"

"Hear! Hear!" agreed Mr Brown. "What do you say, Paddington?"

"It was very nice," said Paddington, licking some cream from his whiskers. "Except I had a bone in my Christmas pudding."

"You *what*?" exclaimed Mrs Brown. "Don't be silly – there are no bones in Christmas pudding."

"I had one," said Paddington, firmly. "It was all hard – and it stuck in my throat."

"Good gracious!" exclaimed Mrs Bird. "The five pence! I always put a piece of silver in the Christmas pudding."

"What!" said Paddington, nearly falling off his chair. "A five pence? I've never heard of a five pence pudding before."

"Quick," shouted Mr Brown, rising to the emergency. "Turn him upside down."

Before Paddington could reply, he found himself hanging head downwards while Mr Brown and Mr Gruber took it in turns to shake him. The rest of the family stood round watching the floor.

"It's no good," said Mr Brown, after a while. "It must have gone too far." He helped Mr Gruber lift Paddington into an armchair, where he lay gasping for breath.

"I've got a magnet upstairs," said Jonathan. "We could try lowering it down his throat on a piece of string."

"I don't think so, dear," said Mrs Brown, in a worried tone of voice. "He might swallow that and then we should be even worse off." She bent over the chair. "How do you feel, Paddington?"

"Sick," said Paddington, in an aggrieved tone of voice.

"Of course you do, dear," said Mrs Brown. "It's only to be expected. There's only one thing to do – we shall have to send for the doctor."

"Thank goodness I scrubbed it first," said Mrs Bird. "It might have been covered with germs."

"But I *didn't* swallow it," gasped Paddington. "I only nearly did. Then I put it on the side of my plate. I didn't know it was five pence because it was all covered with Christmas pudding."

Paddington felt very fed up. He'd just eaten one of the best dinners he could ever remember and now he'd been turned upside down and shaken without even being given time to explain.

Everyone exchanged glances and then crept quietly away, leaving Paddington to recover by himself. There didn't seem to be much they *could* say.

But after the dinner things had been cleared away, and by the time Mrs Bird had made some strong coffee, Paddington was almost himself again. He was sitting up in the chair helping himself to some dates when they trooped back into the room. It took a lot to make Paddington ill for very long.

When they had finished their coffee, and were sitting round the blazing fire feeling warm and comfortable, Mr Brown rubbed his hands. "Now, Paddington," he said, "it's not only Christmas, it's your birthday as well. What would you like to do?"

A mysterious expression came over Paddington's face. "If you all go in the other room," he announced, "I've a special surprise for you."

"Oh dear, *must* we, Paddington?" said Mrs Brown. "There isn't a fire."

"I shan't be long," said Paddington, firmly. "But it's a special surprise and it has to be prepared." He held the door open and the Browns, Mrs Bird, and Mr Gruber filed obediently into the other room.

"Now close your eyes," said Paddington, when they were all settled, "and I'll let you know when I'm ready."

Mrs Brown shivered. "I hope you won't be too long," she called. But the only reply was the sound of the door clicking shut.

They waited for several minutes without speaking, and then Mr Gruber cleared his throat. "Do you think young Mr Brown's forgotten about us?" he asked.

"I don't know," said Mrs Brown. "But I'm not waiting much longer."

"Henry!" she exclaimed, as she opened her eyes. "Have you gone to sleep?"

"Er, wassat?" snorted Mr Brown. He had eaten such a large dinner he was finding it difficult to keep awake. "What's happening? Have I missed anything?"

"Nothing's happening," said Mrs Brown. "Henry, you'd better go and see what Paddington's up to."

Several more minutes went by before Mr Brown returned to announce that he couldn't find Paddington anywhere.

"Well, he must be *somewhere*," said Mrs Brown. "Bears don't disappear into thin air."

"Crikey!" exclaimed Jonathan, as a thought suddenly struck him. "You don't think he's playing at Father Christmas, do you? He was asking all about it the other day when he put his list up the chimney. I bet that's why he wanted us to come in here – because this chimney connects with the one upstairs – and there isn't a fire."

"Father Christmas?" said Mr Brown. "I'll give him Father Christmas!" He stuck his head up the chimney and called Paddington's name several times. "I can't see anything," he said, striking a match. As if in answer a large lump of soot descended and burst on top of his head.

"Now look what you've done, Henry," said Mrs Brown. "Shouting so – you've disturbed the soot. All over your clean shirt!"

"If it is young Mr Brown, perhaps he's stuck somewhere," suggested Mr Gruber. "He did have rather a large dinner. I remember wondering at the time where he put it all."

Mr Gruber's suggestion had an immediate effect on the party and everyone began to look serious.

"Why, he might suffocate with the fumes," exclaimed Mrs Bird, as she hurried out to the broom cupboard.

When she returned, armed with a mop, everyone took it in turns to poke it up the chimney but even though they strained their ears they couldn't hear a sound.

It was while the excitement was at its height that Paddington came into the room. He looked most surprised when he saw Mr Brown with his head up the chimney.

"You can come into the dining-room now," he announced, looking round the room. "I've finished wrapping my presents and they're all on the Christmas tree."

"You don't mean to say," spluttered Mr Brown, as he sat in the fireplace rubbing his face with a handkerchief, "you've been in the other room all the time?"

"Yes," said Paddington, innocently, "I hope I didn't keep you waiting too long."

Mrs Brown looked at her husband. "I thought you said you'd looked everywhere," she exclaimed.

"Well – we'd just come from the dining-room," said Mr Brown, looking very sheepish. "I didn't think he'd be *there*."

"It only goes to show," said Mrs Bird hastily, as she caught sight of the expression on Mr Brown's face, "how easy it is to give a bear a bad name."

Paddington looked most interested when they explained to him what all the fuss was about.

"I never thought of coming down the chimney," he said, staring at the fireplace.

"Well, you're not thinking about it now either," replied Mr Brown sternly.

But even Mr Brown's expression changed as he followed Paddington into the dining-room and saw the surprise that had been prepared for them.

In addition to the presents that had already been placed on the tree, there were now six newly wrapped ones tied to the lower branches. If the Browns recognised the wrapping paper they had used for Paddington's presents earlier in the day, they were much too polite to say anything.

"I'm afraid I had to use old paper," said Paddington apologetically, as he waved a paw at the tree. "I hadn't any money left. That's why you had to go in the other room while I wrapped them."

"Really, Paddington," said Mrs Brown. "I'm very cross with you – spending all your money on presents for us."

"I'm afraid they're rather ordinary," said Paddington, as he settled back in a chair to watch the others. "But I hope you like them. They're all labelled so that you know which is which."

"Ordinary?" exclaimed Mr Brown as he opened his parcel. "I don't call a pipe rack ordinary. And there's an ounce of my favourite tobacco tied to the back as well!"

"Gosh! A new stamp album!" cried Jonathan. "Whizzo! And it's got some stamps inside already."

"They're Peruvian ones from Aunt Lucy's postcards," said Paddington. "I've been saving them for you."

"And I've got a box of paints," exclaimed Judy. "Thank you very much, Paddington. It's just what I wanted."

"We all seem to be lucky," said Mrs Brown, as she unwrapped a parcel containing a bottle of her favourite lavender water. "How *did* you guess? I finished my last bottle only a week ago."

"I'm sorry about your parcel, Mrs Bird," said Paddington, looking across the room. "I had a bit of a job with the knots."

"It must be something special," said Mr Brown. "It seems all string and no parcel."

"That's because it's really a clothes-line," explained Paddington, "not string. I rescued it when I got stuck in the revolving doors at Crumbold & Ferns."

"That makes two presents in one," said Mrs Bird, as she freed the last of the knots and began unwinding yards and yards of paper. "How exciting. I can't think what it can be.

"Why," she exclaimed. "I do believe it's a brooch! And it's shaped like a bear – how lovely!" Mrs Bird looked most touched as she handed the present round for everyone to see. "I shall keep it in a safe place," she added, "and only wear it on special occasions – when I want to impress people."

"I don't know what mine is," said Mr Gruber, as they all turned to him. He squeezed the parcel. "It's such a funny shape.

"It's a drinking mug!" he exclaimed, his face lighting up with pleasure. "And it even has my name painted on the side!"

"It's for your elevenses, Mr Gruber," said Paddington. "I noticed your old one was getting rather chipped."

"I'm sure it will make my cocoa taste better than it ever has before," said Mr Gruber.

He stood up and cleared his throat. "I think I would like to offer a vote of thanks to young Mr Brown," he said, "for all his nice presents. I'm sure he must have given them a great deal of thought."

"Hear! Hear!" echoed Mr Brown, as he filled his pipe.

Mr Gruber felt under his chair. "And while I think of it, Mr Brown, I have a small present for you."

Everyone stood round and watched while Paddington struggled with his parcel, eager to see what Mr Gruber had bought him. A gasp of surprise went up as he tore the paper to one side, for it was a beautifully bound leather scrapbook, with 'Paddington Brown' printed in gold leaf on the cover.

Paddington didn't know what to say, but Mr Gruber waved his thanks to one side. "I know how you enjoy writing about your adventures, Mr Brown," he said. "And you have so many I'm sure your present scrapbook must be almost full."

"It is," said Paddington, earnestly. "And I'm sure I shall have lots more. Things happen to me, you know. But I shall only put my best ones in here!"

When he made his way up to bed later that evening, his mind was in such a whirl, and he was so full of good things, he could hardly climb the stairs – let alone think about anything. He wasn't quite sure which he had enjoyed most. The presents, the Christmas dinner, the games, or the tea – with the special marmalade-layer birthday cake Mrs Bird had made in his honour. Pausing on the corner half way up, he decided he had enjoyed giving his own presents best of all.

"Paddington! Whatever have you got there?" He jumped and hastily hid his paw behind his back as he heard Mrs Bird calling from the bottom of the stairs.

"It's only some five pence pudding, Mrs Bird," he called, looking over the banisters guiltily. "I thought I might get hungry during the night and I didn't want to take any chances."

"Honestly!" Mrs Bird exclaimed, as she was joined by the others. "What does that bear look like? A paper hat about ten sizes too big on his head – Mr Gruber's scrapbook in one paw – and a plate of Christmas pudding in the other!"

"I don't care what he looks like," said Mrs Brown, "so long as he stays that way. The place wouldn't be the same without him."

But Paddington was too far away to hear what was being said. He was already sitting up in bed, busily writing in his scrapbook.

First of all, there was a very important notice to go on the front page. It said: PADINGTUN BROWN,

32 WINDSOR GARDENS,

LUNDUN,

ENGLAND,

YUROPE,

THE WORLD.

Then, on the next page he added, in large capital letters: MY ADDVENTURES. CHAPTER WUN.

Paddington sucked his pen thoughtfully for a moment and then carefully replaced the top on the bottle of ink before it had a chance to fall over on the sheets. He felt much too sleepy to write any more. But he didn't really mind. Tomorrow was another day – and he felt quite sure he *would* have some more adventures – even if he didn't know what they were going to be as yet.

Paddington lay back and pulled the blankets up round his whiskers. It was warm and comfortable and he sighed contentedly as he closed his eyes. It was nice being a bear. Especially a bear called Paddington.